ACCIDENTALLY KIDNAPPING THE MAFIA BOSS

EVIE ROSE

Copyright © 2025 by Evie Rose

All rights reserved.

No part of this book may be reproduced in any form or by any electronic or mechanical means, including information storage and retrieval systems, without written permission from the author, except for the use of brief quotations in a book review.

This story is a work of fiction. Names, characters, places, and incidents are the product of the author's imagination or are used fictitiously. Any resemblance to actual events, locales, or persons, living or dead, is coincidental.

Cover: © 2025 by Cormar Covers.

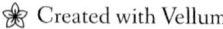 Created with Vellum

1

MILLIE

This is the stupidest thing I've ever done for my brother, and that includes when I cut his hair because he said he wanted it shorter, and he ended up looking like he had a cartoon hedgehog camping on his head. Thankfully, that grew out. Unfortunately, he's not ten years old now, and I need someone who's good at cutting debt, not hair.

Admittedly, Noah didn't say he wanted to be handcuffed, bundled into my car, and removed from London. But the cuffs are furry, so they won't hurt him.

My brother will be furious that they're pink though.

Taking a deep breath, I check everything is as ready as it's going to be. I've left the car door open, and I'm behind the back exit of the pub.

Noah leaves his bar work job at this time, and I come and meet him and walk him home when I'm worried if I'm not there he'll decide to go to a casino instead. That's every night now, unless I'm working. But it's only a few streets to the apartment we share so when he sees my car, he's going to know something is up.

I don't want to go into the pub to get him. I really cannot risk seeing Noah's boss and drooling all over him. Again.

Finn Kilburn might have movie-star good looks, a smooth Irish accent, and billions in the bank, but he's scary. He's drug-laced hot chocolate, so divine you wouldn't even care as you slipped into the darkness.

And the one time we met, I turned into a zombie. *Must eat brains...* Well. Not that exactly. His brain is not what I'd like to wrap my mouth around, not least because it's terrifyingly sharp. He's known in London as the Playboy Kingpin of Kilburn, but he clearly goes after what he wants. That inspired this intervention I'm doing with my brother, actually. I could tell he assumed I'd be another notch on his bedpost and all his intoxicating energy was focused on getting me into a place where I would inevitably submit to anything he wanted.

And I could feel the tug. If I conceded, I knew I'd be lost. He'd take me home, and I'd never recover. I'd be obsessed with him for life.

I was so torn at that moment, because I wanted to do as he said and forget all my responsibilities.

Then it occurred to me: if I could get Noah away, somewhere out of London, perhaps I could channel that mesmerising green-eyed, suited, charismatic Irish-kingpin energy and get my brother on the straight and narrow again.

Hence, I am staging a Kingpin Inspired Intervention of Life Logistics. I'm not sure I've got that acronym right yet, but kidnap doesn't sound great either.

I ping Noah a message that I'm outside, then wait, slipping my phone back into my pocket and readying the pink furry handcuffs.

There's a set of two steps from the door, and I'm to the

side, so when it finally opens and my heart makes a bid to quit this plan the rest of me is enacting, via my throat, all I get is a sense of height. He feels even taller than usual.

My little brother.

I give him a shove as he pauses, no doubt confused to see my car, and not me.

He stumbles, and in a second I've grabbed one of his hands—he's bigger in the dark somehow—and then the other and yanked it behind him and into the cuffs.

Finn.

For a moment all my instincts say this isn't my brother, and instead is the scary and gorgeous kingpin. But that's crazy, part of the illusions of seeing Finn Kilburn for the last week, and feeling myself being watched.

I push the thought away.

"It's Millie," I whisper. "It's alright."

Then I shove him into the back seat of the car, where his torso hits the springy cushions and he lets out an "Ooof". He goes in easily. Of course he does. He's my brother, and he knows I won't hurt him.

But then he's rolling over and kicking out.

OMG how does he have so many long legs? Did he transform into a spider while I wasn't watching?

"Just trust me," I say panickily. I shove his feet into the car, repeatedly, squeaking with frustration and slamming the door behind him.

Noah is going to be so angry with me.

Whelp.

I rush around but as soon as I'm in the front seat, he's already sitting up and flicking the handle.

"It's got the child lock on," I tell him, and start the engine. "You can't get out."

I drive off, my heart hammering.

Noah doesn't say anything, but I hear a deep sigh. A glance in the rear-view mirror reveals his head is bowed so I can't see his face because it's in the shadows.

"I'm really sorry."

This gets a grunt.

Yeah. Definitely the pink handcuffs are the issue.

That and the abduction.

I steel myself. This is the right thing to do, even if it feels like yet another heavy responsibility that I've taken on for my family.

I wait for Noah's outrage, but nothing comes. The silence is thick. Maybe it's the knowledge that I'm doing something about my problems rather than allowing life to just happen, but for once, I don't feel alone. This is way better than coming home to an empty apartment and microwaving a meal for one while Noah is out gambling. Though he's being surly and silent, and there'll be a confrontation when he discovers I'm taking him to our parents' cottage, I have an unexpected warm blanket of confidence around my shoulders.

This will work out.

I think it went pretty well for my first kidnap.

"You don't want to ask where we're going?" I ask, aiming for a light tone.

No reply.

"Your gambling is out of hand, Noah. Sorry, but it is." My voice wobbles and I channel my inner kingpin. I half expect a barrage of angry denials. But no. Nothing.

A *grunt*.

Another stupid grunt, and irritation flares in me. All my feckless brother gives me is a wordless answer that could be anything, or anyone. Honestly.

I roll my eyes as I turn my small car onto the motorway and head north.

Maybe when it's light, and he sees the pink handcuffs, he'll talk.

I sigh. "It's a good thing I love you."

2

FINN

ONE WEEK EARLIER

The pub is full to bursting as I walk in, but as ever it instantly goes quiet. I almost sigh. It's been a long time since I could enter unnoticed. I've got my core team of six men with me this evening, but it's not them that cause the hush that's broken only by the beat of the music and the whispers and giggles of the women who blush and look over.

Nope, it's me.

Or rather, it's the man I pretend I still am.

I wink at the woman next to me, who's with a guy who bristles but knows better than to say anything to the kingpin of Kilburn.

A man behind me gives a belly laugh. "Finn, you dirty dog."

Nodding and catching the eye of another woman is second nature to me, but I don't hold her gaze for long.

Right, duty done, playboy reputation upheld. Now I can get on with business.

Ronan has gone to clear out the table at the back with the best line of sight to the whole room, and I prowl through the crowd, which parts for me, as natural as the hush settling in a forest as a wolf stalks through. But they also greet me nervously, eager to please.

"Hi Finn!"

"Hey, Finn, how you doing?"

"Alright," I acknowledge them. I nod and smile and flirt a little.

How is it possible to feel so fecking lonely when surrounded by people who are desperate to be your friend? I guess I really am one of a kind despite looking just like my family, because I can manage it here in any of my London territory's pubs, in Ireland, or with the men who work under me in the Kilburn mafia.

It's as though wherever I go or whatever I do, there's something missing.

"Richmond is here," Cormac mutters to me, peering over his shoulder.

"Bring them in," I instruct him.

Cormac nods and doubles back, finding it considerably more difficult to return through the crowd of partygoers than it was to follow in my wake.

I take a seat on one side of the large circular table in the corner that Ronan is waiting at, and look across the bar. The room has resumed some sense of normalcy.

Everyone is having a good time, which is exactly as it should be. But my god it makes me empty.

"Kilburn," the kingpin of Richmond says as he arrives with a group of men. I stand and casually smile, shaking his hand and making small talk. We order drinks, and there's more chatter as we go through the social niceties.

Has he heard about the latest childish stunt that Essex

has pulled? It's a safe topic for a still probationary member of the London Mafia Syndicate, and he agrees. We move on to complaining that Westminster is a pain in the arse for going on about wanting to have fewer kidnaps. Then Richmond is getting into the conversation, warming to me and telling me whatever the fuck the kingpin of Angel has done this time. I'm only half listening, but it's almost certain the Bratva boss lost his cool and shot someone. That's the Dark Angel's brand.

I want to get this over with and not linger. While like any Kilburn pub, this place has great craic, I'd honestly prefer to be tucked up in bed alone. Pick a girl to pretend to take with me and then put her in a taxi, fake some crisis to attend to, or make a play of being totally scuttered from too much whiskey. The usual things.

Most of the people in the pub are half my age, and drawn by my power and money, as well as the legendary Kilburn charm. And they're all...

Except, no.

There's one girl across the bar, who doesn't fit. Big, anxious blue eyes. Honey blonde hair in a neat ponytail, and a too large jacket covers her shoulders. She's trying to get the attention of the barman, and failing.

As though she can feel my gaze, she looks right at me, and our eyes lock.

My cock surges, feeling like she's put her hand on it.

She's beautiful. The sort of under-rated beauty that goes unnoticed amongst the expensive clothes and makeup of the women around her.

The bolt of recognition is lightning.

She looks as out of place as I feel, and her expression echoes what's in my chest precisely. There's so much weight on her shoulders, it's as though she's being dragged down by it. Her eyes hold something soft and bleak. Worry, and no way to stem it.

"Ronan," I cut into Richmond's story with a summons for my fixer. This is the girl I'll woo and flirt with and take home. And I don't think I'll be putting her in a taxi. No. She'll be in my bed, all night long.

First time in years.

"Boss." He's at my side immediately.

"Invite the girl at the bar with the blonde ponytail to join me."

He hesitates. "The one in the jacket?"

He's doubly confused, because it's been years since I pulled this sort of move during a work meeting, and a girl in a coat isn't the type I usually select.

"Yes," I snap. "Now."

Before she leaves. She can't leave.

"The Playboy Kingpin strikes again," Richmond drawls, the note of "I'm not impressed with you" clear and dangerous as a shard of glass in a bar brawl.

Feck. A partnership with Richmond will bring money and power to Kilburn and all who live here, and cement my place in the London Mafia Syndicate. I need him on-side.

But my cock is still tingling in a way it hasn't for a long time.

I might need that girl more.

"Everyone has their vices, Richmond," I say, leaning back in a deliberately arrogant and dismissive gesture. As though my action was incidental. It's better if Richmond isn't aware of this girl's significance to me. We're allies now, but that doesn't mean there isn't danger with any mafia interaction.

This girl is different, I feel it in my bones. But no one can know that.

Richmond narrows his eyes. "The goods we talked about. What's your best price?"

Jesus. So, he's going to insult me by crassly starting with money talk before we've finished our drinks. "Are you enjoying the whiskey? It's good stuff."

My gaze returns to the girl at the bar. Ronan is talking to her, but it doesn't seem it's going well. My heart thuds.

"You know it's very nice, Kilburn, what do you want for it?" Richmond's accent is posh, and irritated.

"Well, it depends on how much you take, and how much you like it." I reluctantly drag my eyes back to Richmond. "And if we're friends on a continuing basis, I can do you a better..."

Like the girl is a magnet and I'm base metal, I glance across at her and promptly lose my train of thought when I see that she's still there and Ronan isn't.

What?

"Deal?" Richmond growls.

"What fecking happened?" I demand as Ronan approaches.

"She uh." My fixer looks terrified. "She said no, Boss."

No?!

She said, no? To me? The dark creature in my chest roars.

"Excuse me." I'm on my feet in a second.

Despite the music and the people, my little prey spots me out of the corner of her eye, the whites showing stark even in the low light.

"Is this seat taken?" It's not quite a question to the man in the barstool next to my girl, and the bloke scrambles to vacate it.

The girl opens her mouth, as though to protest.

I take the angel in from head to toe. She's wearing jeans under a shapeless coat, and her hair is in a messy fall over her shoulder. Her cheeks are dotted with freckles I want to kiss.

"Will you let me buy you a drink, pet?" The endearment is out before I can think better of it.

Pet. An Irish word for a loved one.

I've never used it before for a woman. Or anyone. I'm known as a player and a rogue, charming, but not a man who uses cute nicknames. I've always felt that would be insincere.

She shakes her head, but her gaze takes me in like she can't look away. Her little plump lips are a perfect "o". "I'm just waiting for someone."

"A boyfriend?" I snarl.

I hope not, for everyone's sake. I'd break the neck of a man who was between her and me.

But she flushes, her cheeks pinkening.

So pretty. So fecking pretty.

"I need to speak to my brother, then I'm going," she mutters.

"Who's your brother?" I follow her gaze to one of the barmen. "Ah, Noah."

She jolts. "You know him?"

"You could say that," I say dryly. I'm his boss. I know all my staff. "I'm Finn, by the way."

The colour promptly drains from her face and for the first time in my life, I regret everything that I am.

Notorious womaniser from my younger years. A billionaire and a businessman, yes, and also a mafia boss who deals in power and blood and illegal trade.

If this girl would look at me again like she did from across the room before she knew my name, shyly curious, I'd give it all up in a heartbeat. I'd rewind time and be a better man, knowing it was worth the wait for her.

But I can't though.

She's clearly much younger than me, and that makes me wretched. I should fund research into a time machine, or some anti-ageing shite. I should walk away, and leave her to her innocence.

I don't think I can.

"You're the kingpin of Kilburn." She swallows the last word.

"And you are...?"

"Millie."

The name I will be repeating as I orgasm tonight is cute.

"Grand to meet you," I manage to say. How can I get her home with me, right away? Normally, I have smooth words. I've even used cheesy pick-up lines or outright demands with perfect success. If I crooked my finger, they came.

Except this girl.

It has never mattered before, and now it does. I have no charm. No moves.

"What do you do?" I ask, like a lemon.

"I'm a nurse." Her gaze flicks between me and her brother, who is serving a customer. He's an unassuming guy, but I suddenly have reason to check up on him.

"He'll be off shift in a couple of hours. Come and have a drink with me while you wait." I glance across at Richmond. His expression is thunder.

Fine. I can do without the London Mafia Syndicate. It seemed fun and profitable, but so is starring in porn, and I'm not going to do that either.

"I can't... I have to..." An expression I don't understand

crosses her face. Some sort of distress. "I have to talk with him."

"What's the matter?" I suppress the urge to raise my hand and get her brother over with a snap of my fingers. I don't want her running off, and I need to hear why she's upset, so I can fix it. "Tell me."

"No, it..." She pauses, and an idea dawns on her, as transparent as the morning sky. "Maybe I shouldn't. I won't..."

"*What is it?*" My voice goes low and firm, like when I'm demanding answers from one of my men.

"I thought I should tell him off for something..." She bites her pretty, plush bottom lip.

"Tell him off for what?" I demand. I can't help her if I don't understand what the issue is, and if I'm wrecking the whole deal with Richmond for this girl, I need to know everything.

"But actually, it'll be better not to right now. I'll speak to him about it when... Can you not let him know I was here?" She slides from the stool and my heart clenches at how tiny she is compared to me. Five-foot and a bit to my six-foot-five.

"I won't tell him, but—"

"I have to go." She's already moving away, and I clench my fist to prevent myself from snatching her to me. Can't scare my pet.

"Stay." My chest tightens. She mustn't go. She hasn't agreed to marry me yet. She hasn't fallen in love with me. I barely know anything about her, but that there's some secret about her and her brother, and my heart is already tattered and bleeding that she's going to be out of reach.

Millie turns her head, and for a long second I'm

convinced she'll sit back down, or come with me to the table.

Then she has bolted away in the crowd, her short height meaning she's immediately swallowed up.

Little Cinderella, running out of the party without leaving so much as I slipper to trace her by.

Thankfully, it's the twenty-first Century. I'm going to find out everything there is to know about Millie. Watch her, protect her, discover all her secrets.

Slowly, I make my way back to Richmond.

"Sorry-sorry-sorry-sorry." I sit down and smile charmingly, though every instinct in me screams that this is irrelevant. She is the only thing that matters. Millie.

"Very young, isn't she?" Richmond's lip curls. "Your bit of skirt more important than—"

I have my gun pointed at the other mafia boss' head before he can finish his remark. Around us there's the click of safeties as every man draws.

Anger pulses through me.

"You will not disrespect her," I grind out. She is too young for me, and a sheen of oily guilt makes my temper burn hotter. "And you will take that back or it will be the last thing you say, the Syndicate be damned."

Richmond tilts his chin up, and views me appraisingly for a few long seconds, and I think about the war I might have just started.

"I take it back." He nods slowly. "My apologies."

Blood still pounds around my body, but I lower my gun, and everyone else follows suit.

There's a short silence, then Richmond's mouth quirks up. "You'll fit in with the London Mafia Syndicate exceedingly well. Let's talk about a long-term deal."

Feck, I didn't expect that.

As we thrash out the details, Richmond's noticeably warmer towards me, but all I can think about is Millie. And how to make her *mine*.

3

FINN

Now

"It's a good thing I love you."

She's not saying that to me, but feck... If she was, I'd reply that I love her too, more than anything in the world. I love her with the lusty energy of Irish grass and the deep intensity of the stormy sea, despite having barely met her. Apparently when you meet your soulmate, you just know.

"This is for the best," she tells me. Or Noah. "You'll see."

Easing myself back, I slide to the side and ensure my face isn't lit by the streetlights as I make myself comfortable.

"You've been gambling so much, I'm surprised you're still employed."

And yeah, she's right. Her brother has been a problem. Though, to be fair, I've been a touch distracted myself recently. And it happens that I have some sympathy with obsessions that are unhealthy.

"I'm sorry that your job is going to be at risk since you're not turning up for work tomorrow. I'll phone the pub and explain. Maybe they'll understand?"

I consider interrupting her. There are a number of points that she's very wrong on, and that she thinks I'm her brother is not even the most significant.

She thinks she has kidnapped someone who doesn't want to be here, and that she has to save her brother. When in fact, I'm all too eager to be with her, and I've dealt with her brother.

Ever since I first saw her across the bar in one of the many Kilburn pubs I own, I've been compelled to find out everything about her. Following her hasn't been enough. Befriending her brother, who is a decent guy with a gambling addiction and a lot to learn. Checking on her at her work at the hospital. I've been looking for a way to get further into her life, and what she doesn't know is that we were going to talk tonight, and she'd have come home with me, even if she hadn't made this reckless move.

I love that she did this for me. For us.

"I met your boss the other day."

The air is sucked from my lungs.

"He seemed..."

She pauses.

It takes everything in me not to reach over the seat and demand she continue speaking.

"I dunno. He's a mafia boss, but I didn't die." She laughs a bit. "People say he's a charming playboy with a side of psychosis, but he was..." That thought gets left unfinished, but there's a note of wistfulness in her tone that gives me hope. "Maybe he'll keep your barman position open, or give you another."

His job is safe, and it physically hurts to not be able to reassure her on that point.

"It's a long drive if you won't talk to me," she interrupts my thoughts. "You're not going to ask where we're going?"

I am curious about that, and the edge to her voice suggests her brother would have guessed.

"Nothing, Noah?"

She'd be as fierce a mother as any Irish Mammy. She'd be a queen by my side, and I bet she'd be a minx in my bed. I'd already wanted Millie, but now? So much more.

A decent man would tell her everything, and save her the drive to wherever we're going.

But I have been an amoral bastard from birth, the son of a bad man and stubborn woman. But they're all in Ireland, and sometimes I feel that lack of family.

Recently more than ever.

It's since I met Millie. She brings out all the longing for connection rather than more money and power.

There's a silence, and I fill the time with the fun little challenge of getting the cuffs off. Pretty straightforward, since she didn't do them up tight. Soft-hearted.

They're fecking fur lined, which is adorable.

"We're going to the beach cottage for a week…" That must mean something to Noah, as she doesn't elaborate.

But a house by the sea sounds excellent. And small will be ideal for us. Somewhere Millie and I can get to know each other? This couldn't be better if I'd planned it myself.

"It'll be our last trip." Her voice trembles. "I don't think I could bear to come to Northumberland and not go to the cottage."

I wrack my brains for where we're going. Northumberland is on the East coast of England, just before you get to Scotland, I think.

"We have to sell it," she says eventually. "Because of

your gambling debts. This is what your addiction has done, Noah. This is why I've asked you, and begged you."

What? Noah said he had loans, and I arranged for them to be paid, of course. But my sweet pet is making this sacrifice? She's amazing.

"Are you not even going to reply?" she says, with a touch of annoyance.

I keep my head low and shake it. No.

Not because I don't feel anything, I do. But because she's talking to me, and I don't want that to stop.

"Our *parents'* cottage. It's all we have left of them, and you took it from us."

My poor pet. I'll fix this for her, of course I will, just as I'd sort everything she let me.

"Are you not even going to say you're sorry?"

I should have guessed Millie would have done what was needed to help her brother. My chest aches for her. So strong, despite being tiny. I'd love to see her use that resilience to deal with more pleasurable challenges, not debt and heartbreak. That strength would be perfect for a mafia boss' wife.

For my wife.

Would she let me give her a family? I'd like that a lot. Her brother is a gobshite, and she deserves better.

She falls silent again, and eventually sighs deeply.

"You might as well sleep."

As she directs, I lie down. But I don't sleep. Just listening to her breathing, catching the scent of her apple shampoo, and feeling her presence close by is soothing in a way I've never felt before.

I think forward to when we stop.

She's going to freak out. She accidentally kidnapped the kingpin in control of the part of London she lives in. I have the luxury of being able to plan, and I need to, since a smart girl like her will try to run from me.

I tried charm and seduction when we met, but she's drained me of any ability to think in her presence. I'm just a morally-grey kingpin, standing before a girl almost half his age, asking her to love him.

Not likely.

But if I insisted. If she thought I was exactly the sort of deadly mafia boss she took me for when I told her my name...

The seed of an idea sprouts and flourishes. What if I turn this kidnapping around? Would she forgive me?

Probably. Orgasms can wear a person down.

She turns on the radio after a while, and apologises. But it only takes a few songs before she's singing along to Taylor Swift and I'm lying on my back, grinning.

Listening to her is a new joy. I've watched from afar, and kept track of her via a hidden app on her phone that her brother kindly and inadvertently passed on when he messaged her. Being close and hearing her voice fills my tattered soul.

I've never been kidnapped before. I've been missing out.

This is the most fun I've had in years.

4

MILLIE

As I drive up the rough gravel track, the horizon opens, and my chest expands. Then there's the line of blue on blue where the ocean meets the sky, with streaks of cloud and seagulls wheeling overhead. A light breeze shakes the spindly grasses growing at the edge of the beach, and the sun is gleaming white as dawn creeps up behind us.

This place is a bittersweet memory of childhood. Being neglected, feral kids was a good thing in the long summer break when we spent all day making sandcastles and playing in the waves or the woods beyond the sand dunes.

The track turns and leads to the side of the cottage, and I draw to a halt in the little parking space. Noah still hasn't sat up. He has totally ignored me since dawn, presumably asleep.

"I'll be back in min," I choke out, then throw myself from the car without looking around at him. Noah's annoyed, I'm sure. Who wouldn't be after being cuffed and kidnapped? Never mind how furious and difficult this week is going to be while I try to straighten him out.

Will a week be long enough? I push that fear aside. It

has to be. And though I don't have much time, I need a moment to myself before I start this self-imposed job. Just an opportunity to have a pee and brace myself.

There's a nick of pain as I let myself into the cottage. This will be my last visit here, and I somehow doubt that helping my brother overcome addiction is going to be a cheery farewell.

I take in the familiar surroundings. The cottage is tiny, just two rooms upstairs and a bathroom that has seashells and white wooden boards with dusky-blue tiles. It's perfectly clean since the fab local lady we employ—employed—has sorted everything after the last rental guests. When I've washed my hands, I check the kitchen cupboards and fridge, and it's all ready. Plenty of fresh fruit and veg, some protein and cupboard basics, plus bags of good microwavable stuff to munch on when we don't want to cook, and the waffle maker I bought a few years ago. The perfect indulgent, quick hot food.

We're all set for what I know will be a difficult week, but I'm certain we can change the life of the man I kidnapped, because I care about him. He's my only family, even if he has messed up.

That doesn't mean it's going to be easy.

Back outside, I breathe in the clean scent of the sea and ignore the butterflies in my tummy. I love it here. So, so much. It's beautiful, wild, and untamed.

"Alright! Wakey-wakey!" I approach my car with false chirpiness. "Ready for your beach holiday? Very wholesome!" I pull open the door and look down.

It's empty. My heart drops through to my feet.

"What?"

He must have crawled over the seats and got out from the front. As I turn, both my hands are snatched in strong fingers, and yanked back in a move I recognise from learning in a video, and using last night. There's the snap of metal and I gasp. Soft handcuffs tighten on my wrists before I can jerk away.

"Well?" says a deep voice from behind me. An Irish accent that's smooth as butter but dark as the bottom of the ocean.

Adrenaline spikes out from my chest, down my arms and legs. I'm shaking as I twist around, eyes wide. And I look right at... Broad shoulders, covered with a rumpled forest-green shirt and charcoal suit jacket.

My heart smashes against my ribs as I tip my head back, up and up, over his open collar, past gleaming silver necklaces, to a short beard. Until I'm looking into a pair of eyes that are such a bright green they seem poisonous in the pale, sparkling morning light reflecting from the sea.

Finn Kilburn.

The blood drains from me like the tide pulling back.

My mouth falls open and is dry as sand. Fear shoots down every limb, vivid and hot.

It immobilises me.

He's as gorgeous as I remember, and my memory has been extremely active since we met. But in the low light of the pub, I didn't see the details that make him all the sexier. The scar over his generous top lip that I couldn't help wanting to kiss. His outrageously long black eyelashes. The distinct lump of his Adam's apple, and the whorls in his stubble.

And he looks furious.

I'm shaking.

I'm caught by my brother's boss. Finn Kilburn is *dangerous* and his silence and the way he's staring at me prickles my skin. The Irish Kilburn kingpin is charming but deadly, and he seems a bit crazy right now, his eyes glittering as he examines me.

"Where's Noah?" I croak.

"I came out to tell you that your brother couldn't come home tonight." Finn raises one dark eyebrow. It has a nick in it. Another scar.

Oh my god. I think... I may have forced the billionaire mafia boss of the London territory where I live into the back of my car, and took him to a seaside cottage.

I abducted the wrong man. Not just a mistake. An absolute *disaster*.

Possibly a fatal one.

"I'm so sorry." The words stumble out. "I didn't mean to, honestly. I'm really so sorry. Please don't hurt me."

I should run. I cast my gaze around. We're in the middle of nowhere, a very long walk to the local village, never mind anywhere that might help me. The isolation is what makes the cottage so tranquil, and perfect for Noah's enforced recuperation.

Even so, I eye up the dunes. Could I get ahead?

"Don't even think about running. I'll catch you."

Heat floods between my legs, and I gasp. Looking back at Finn, his face is like thunder.

It shouldn't be hot.

He'd be faster than me. There's no point in trying to escape, and yet, the instinct to do so is there anyway.

"I'm really sorry." I wince again.

"Are you?" he asks, regarding me from head to toe in a way that makes me flush to the tips of my hair in its sensible ponytail.

"Yes! I meant to kidnap my brother!" Where is Noah? I almost ask. But he's probably fine. Likely made his way home on his own, maybe via the bookies. He'll assume I'm asleep. Or if he notices I'm not at our tiny apartment in Kilburn, he'll think I'm on shift at the hospital.

We often miss each other because of my weird job timing. I gulp.

It could be days until he even realises I'm gone. And then how would he find me? No one knows I'm here.

I'm stuck alone, with a powerful mafia boss who is known for laughing while he kills people. But Finn Kilburn is not smiling right now. He's looking at me with a serious, intent expression.

"You kidnapped me, though."

"Why didn't you tell me?!" I bleat. "That could have prevented this." And probably I'd have been murdered just outside the pub.

At least I got a nice setting for my last breath. Eleven out of ten for planning.

"Are ye victim blaming, now?" he replies in an affronted tone.

"No!" Crap, *no*. What is it about this man that makes me incapable of stringing words together in a normal fashion? "Not at all. Totally my fault. I'm the arsehole. I deserve no donuts..."

I shut my mouth. The "death or donuts" phrase from the Fulham mafia is not the sort of idea I want to put in the kingpin's head.

"But..." he says, rough and inviting.

"I would have stopped. You could have told me," I whisper. Barely audible.

"Wanted to see what you'd do." He shrugs, but his brows are low. "Good craic, too."

"Fun?" Living in Kilburn means I know plenty of Irish words. Being kidnapped is *good craic*? Is he nuts? I think

I'm hyperventilating. I tug at my hands, but they're secure in the cuffs. How did he get out?

"I was in shock, to be sure." The reply is obviously insincere. "Maybe I still am."

"I can help." I'm desperate now. More apologies. That's what's needed. "I'm a nurse. You could unlock me, and I'll check you over, then drive you straight back to Kilburn. No harm done. Can we just forget about this?"

"I will, yeah." His voice drips with sarcasm. "Abducting a mafia boss is no big deal. Zero consequences."

"I'll take you home to London." The more I try to fix this, the more furious he looks. "Right now."

All those things I said in the car... And I sang.

Oh noooo. I sang that song about falling in love and I day-dreamed about this man.

"Think I've spent enough time in your shite car for now," he snaps.

"It's not shite..." I begin and he gives me a dark but somehow pitying look.

"You kidnapped me, pet." His voice goes hard. "You'll have to pay."

An emotion skitters down my spine. Fear, but also excitement, I think? Like a scary movie. "What do you want?"

He looks down at me, gaze lingering on my mouth. A flash of pure arousal lights me up. "Everything."

I bolt.

Barging out of his hold, I head for the beach without even thinking. I make it two steps, then three, and by the fourth I think I might get away. Adrenaline surges.

This is good, right?

Then I'm seat belted by a pair of massive arms and hauled against a solid body. Abdominals, thighs, hard pecs.

"No, you don't." Leaning down, he spins me around, grabs my bottom, and tosses me over his shoulder.

I shriek, and I can't even catch myself as I bounce on his back, only just avoiding face-planting on his arse because my hands are in the cuffs behind me. Then he's walking and I'm staring helplessly at the toned buttocks of the man I accidentally kidnapped.

They are, undeniably, very nice.

5

FINN

I fecking love having Millie over my shoulder. She hardly weighs anything, and her breasts are so good on my lower back they should be illegal. If you could bottle the happiness singing in my blood right now it would sell in Kilburn pubs for thousands a shot. It would make me another billion, but I'd never do it.

Millie is *all mine.*

"Cute place you have here," I comment as I walk around to the front door, hardly even taking a second to admire the sea view.

I have to duck to enter the house—being six-foot-five has its disadvantages—and I'm careful with my pretty little burden as I navigate the old-fashioned small spaces. There's a cute and comfortable snug on one side, with bare stone walls, a log-burning stove, and deep sofas. I turn the other way, into a traditional kitchen with a wooden table and a range cooker that has herbs drying above it.

Selecting the most padded of the chairs, I go to drop Millie from my shoulder, and my hand presses onto her peachy arse, and feck.

Feck.

My cock is solid. I'm filthy to want a girl who's only twenty-two.

It takes me a second to recover as my brain stutters, and I have to drag my palm from that curve to put it at the small of her back. I kneel and set her into the chair, then look straight at her—a novel view when I've been seeing her on a CCTV screen or from the corner of my eye—as she wriggles and peeks out from the hair that pulled out of her ponytail and swung over her eyes when I tossed her upside down.

She watches warily as I reach out, but doesn't draw back. I snag a blonde tendril—it's soft as silk—and brush it behind the shell of her ear. Then the other.

I've got her. She's mine for seven days. And if I have my way, for life.

"What are you going to do?" she asks timidly.

"Let's have a cup of tea first, and we'll see what happens now you're my captive, hmm?"

"I don't want tea, and I don't have any money."

"English hospitality is bollocks," I say, shaking my head.

Her eyes go wide. "Agreed. You could just release me, and save the bother?"

No.

"You created this situation," I point out dryly.

She flicks her gaze to the door surreptitiously, so I go and shut it, locking it with the key she left on the table and pocketing her phone and the car keys as well. That will make it tricky for her to leave, given she's in handcuffs, and I don't want to restrict her too much. Unless it's necessary.

"The key to the cuffs?"

Pressing her lips together, I think for a second she'll refuse.

"In the end pocket of my bag," she admits eventually,

and I correctly identify the pale-blue duffle bag as hers. With her looking on, it feels like an intrusion of privacy as I peer in. Somehow knowing she's observing my obsession makes it feel dirtier than when I was tracking her phone and watching CCTV.

There are white cotton knickers, plain tees, and a sundress. Fuck, I'd love to take her clothes and rub them against my cock like the pervert I am.

But I fish the flimsy little key out and pretend I haven't just fantasised about her as I slide it into my other trouser pocket.

"Are you going to run again?" I ask conversationally as I close the bag and put it aside.

"Yes." Her voice is defiant.

"Don't run." I wink at her. "Let's have breakfast together first." I stand and open the fridge and cupboards, finding utensils and pots and pans, and then find something I didn't expect. I grin.

"Fancy waffles?" I pull out the waffle maker.

Millie blinks at me, then straightens her back. "You want me to make them? You'll need to release my hands."

"Ah no, pet." I like having her at my mercy far too much for that. "How do I know you wouldn't kidnap me again?"

"That's as likely as you rating this cottage five stars in your verified review."

"You could absolutely earn five stars with your hands, pet." She blushes and savage delight rips through me that I've affected her. "But it's not worth the risk," I add. "For a mafia boss to be kidnapped by a pint-sized girl like you once is embarrassing. Twice..."

She snorts.

I'm enjoying this far too much.

Unable to hide my smile, I grab ingredients and find the other items I need from the cupboards.

After a few minutes, and when I have creamy batter in a jug, she mutters, "You really know how to make waffles?"

"Are you doubting my culinary skills as well as depriving me of my liberty?" I pour the mixture into the hot iron.

"You played along!" she protests, not letting me get away with the lie.

Because I think I was half in love with you, and I'm further now because you're smart and sweet and resourceful. And kind—feck—so kind. You were going to help your brother despite him being a fecking eejit.

"A moment of weakness." I'm powerless to resist her. "What if it gets out that you kidnapped me?"

"It won't." She wriggles in the chair.

"My reputation will be shot to bits." I peek at the waffles and the scent of warm, sweet dough fills the air. Perfect.

"I'd never tell anyone!"

"And then there's the issue of compensation," I continue, flipping the golden waffles onto a plate.

"Compensation?" she repeats cautiously.

"You kidnapped me." I scatter the berries on the top, adding a dollop of butter, then drizzling honey over the whole lot.

"I don't have anything to pay you."

"No?" I bring the plates over, and pull up a chair in front of her, the table to the side.

"Didn't you hear me in the car?" she replies with a touch of impatience. "I'm skint. We have to sell this house because my brother is so in debt. I've got nothing."

"Nothing but your beautiful self." I cut a piece of waffle

and spear it with the fork, then offer it to her mouth. "Good thing I don't need money, huh?"

Her gaze pings between my face and the sweet treat I'm offering her.

"Do you like waffles?" I check.

"Yes."

"Me too." We have that in common. See? Soulmates. "So what's the issue here?"

She squirms. "I don't normally have them with so much honey and butter. Lots of sugar is bad—"

I shove the piece of waffle into her mouth to put a stop to such nonsense.

"Do not fecking continue with that thought," I growl as she stares at me in shock. "Eat."

Achingly slowly, she closes her lips and chews. A little mew of pleasure comes from her throat as she swallows.

My cock twitches at the sight of her. The sound she makes is so innocently sexy, I want to eat her whole.

"Good?" I ask, and she presses her lips together, unsure.

Taking another chunk of waffle and berries, I deliberately dip it into the honey and butter.

"Open," I snap when she doesn't respond immediately.

And this time, she does as I say, and her eyelids flutter closed, covering those pale-blue eyes as she enjoys the treat. I don't move my gaze from hers as I eat some myself—enjoying us sharing our food—and cut another piece of waffle ready for her.

She opens her mouth willingly for the next bite, and my cock responds with predictable enthusiasm at the sight of her pink, glistening tongue and soft lips.

I only get harder as she eats more, and it's almost unbearably intimate. The way she's helpless and accepting, I can't help think about what else I could see if she'd like in her mouth while her hands are restrained. Unbidden, the image of standing, undoing my belt, releasing my cock, and gripping her hair to shove my length between those sweet lips of hers, has me leaking pre-come within seconds. The thought of the feel of the back of her throat, fucking her face as she moaned and her eyes watered, until I erupted, and she swallowed it all down like the good girl she is?

Oooof.

Nothing has ever been as perfect as treating her to breakfast, but maybe telling her to suck my cock, and having her greedily take it all, would be.

When I steal mouthfuls of waffle, she watches me with the same intensity as I view her. And yeah, it could be she's trying to escape, but her blown pupils and the way her eyes linger on my open collar. And my hands. She looks again and again at my forearms and the tattoos on my right wrist that are exposed every time I reach out.

The waffles are excessively sweet, with a hint of salt from the butter and I can't help but wonder if she'll taste even better.

"What do you want as payment for your inconvenience?" she asks eventually, as we get to the bottom of the waffle stack.

I'd like you, body and soul. Optional decorative bow as you give yourself to me.

"Sure, look." It's a measure of how much she affects me that I use the Irish phrase that's nothing more than a hesitation device. "I haven't decided yet."

Will a week be long enough for her to fall in love with me? Probably not, given she's a pure little angel, and I'm a blood-stained kingpin who has been stalking her, and is fifteen years her senior.

I cut the last bit of waffle in two and scoop up the honey

and butter pooled on the plate before bringing one piece slowly to my mouth, enjoying how her eyes track my movements.

"Second best way to eat honey," I say with a smirk, hoping she'll understand my implication. "I love sweet and salty."

She blinks at me, not blushing or showing any sign of recognition, and I chuckle. My girl might be a nurse, but she's innocent, it turns out. I'm curious about how inexperienced she is.

Unfortunately, all that attempted seductive-shit backfires, and the sugary liquid drips onto my chin.

Smooth, Finn. Real smooth.

I've lost all my seduction game, and I'd say it was years of women throwing themselves at me and disinterested celibacy, but it's not. It's Millie.

Using my thumb, I catch the droplet and suck the sweetness meaningfully from the pad.

Her breath hitches and I hide my satisfaction by sweeping up all the remaining honey onto the last bit of waffle. It's soaked in it.

"Open your mouth, pet."

"I've had enough," she says with panic in her voice.

"I'll say when you've had enough," I rumble. One more mouthful won't hurt her if she really is full, but I doubt that's the issue.

"It's too much."

"I don't think so." The forkful of honey-covered waffle is beginning to drip and I hold it to her lips. Insistent.

She trembles as she opens her mouth this time, and her breath is uneven as I slide it in, the honey smearing over her lips. It's as slow and sensual as how I'd fuck her for the first time, and a groan reverberates from my chest as she takes what I give her.

The smallest movement risks me coming in my pants like I'm seventeen, not thirty-seven.

Millie makes everything new.

"See, too much sweetness isn't a bad thing." My voice is husky. We're both affected by this.

A drop of honey slides from her lips, and I see her feel it, reaching with that pink tongue... And missing. It tracks down her chin.

"Looks like you're having the same issue as I had," I tease. "Admit you love the sweetness, and I'll help you."

"This isn't fair," she grumbles, pressing her lips together, failing to get the honey. "You could use your hands."

I lean forward and say in a low voice, "You telling me I shouldn't?"

"I'm saying you should release mine."

"Come 'ere to me." And while the phrase just means "listen" in Irish slang, Millie takes it adorably literally, and leans forwards, big eyes gazing up.

"I won't use my hands. That's equal, isn't it?"

I lean across, bringing my face closer and closer. My good, brave girl doesn't back down, but her pupils go big as I draw closer. I examine her closely. Perfect peaches-and-cream complexion, stained with a touch of pink. Cute, button nose. Her lips are a dusky rose-red, and so plump they're made to be kissed. Those freckles I want to taste.

My mouth waters.

Her long pale eyelashes brush up and down as she watches me.

"What are you doing?" she asks as my breath ghosts her cheek.

"Helping you with that honey."

"What?" she protests breathily.

"Without my hands," I explain. Then I tilt my head and give a slow, leisurely lick over her honey-covered chin, all the way to her lips. It's dominant, and carnal, and deliberately showing her that I can do whatever I want with her right now. She's utterly in my control.

She gasps, and lets out a soft little whimper.

I ease back, and I'm gratified to see her chest rising and falling quickly. She's as affected by this chemistry between us as I am.

A satisfied grin tugs at the sides of my mouth. I'm supposed to be playing at being annoyed. Her harsh captor taking revenge. But she's so fecking sweet, there's nothing I wouldn't do for a taste of her everywhere.

I lick my lips.

"Delicious."

6

MILLIE

His gaze drops to my lips, and pure arousal flares in my tummy and between my legs.

He licked me.

And that is not—strictly—the most unhinged thing that has happened today.

I kidnapped a mafia boss. And then, I got kidnapped right back.

Okay, that's sort of on-brand. But then Finn made me breakfast. He fed me the best waffles I've ever eaten, mouthful by mouthful as though he'd like to eat me up. I had no idea food cooked by someone else tasted so good.

And then his tongue, hot and wet and so intimate and… Shocking. Weirdly taboo. My heart is vibrating in my chest, and my breathing is ragged.

I'm wet and squirmy between the legs in a way I've never felt before. Well. Except that night in his pub, when electricity shot down my spine and right to my clit when I saw Finn, like he had reached across the space and run his finger down my body with a hundred volts sparking between us.

Is this what he does to every woman he focuses his attention on? I suppose I'm not special. He is the playboy kingpin, after all.

That thought dampens my excitement, replacing it with wariness.

"What now?" I ask, and my voice shakes.

Wordlessly, he stands and clears away the plate, stashing everything into the dishwasher before flicking it on. Then he opens the bags I brought. One with clothes for me, the other with stuff for my brother.

A crease appears between his brows as he looks at the contents of my brother's bag. Although he's a bit taller and bulkier than Noah—how did I imagine he was Noah? Finn is so much more intimidating—I think they would probably fit him.

He slings the bags over his shoulder, and I hear him taking the steep stairs two at a time, leaving me alone.

This is my chance.

I'm out of the kitchen and at the lounge window in a second, and oh—this is going to be far more difficult than I thought. I reverse in and look over my shoulder, so I can reach the catch. The little key is fussy, and I turn it, heart pounding, then press the handle. Nothing.

Nooo, I just locked it?

I flip it back. Squeeze. It doesn't move.

There's a roaring in my ears. I'm wasting precious time.

Turning the key again, the window opens.

Ahhhgggg! I swear it—no time for frustration, just get on.

I shove the window open with my fingertips and shuffle backwards, sitting on the windowsill and pushing my bottom out to lever the glass further. I peek down, and outside is a scrubby bush. I gulp. This is going to hurt, but a soft landing is a good thing, right?

Quick.

Get away from the dangerous mafia boss, run down the beach until I reach civilisation, phone the police, something-something-something, get to London and everything will magically be alright. Another wriggle, and I look back into the room as my feet kick out to find purchase on something to help me...

Finn is leaning in the doorway, arms crossed, regarding me with an utterly exasperated expression on his gorgeous face.

"I left you for twenty seconds, Millie," he growls.

Oh. Sugar.

I overbalance.

For a sickening moment I'm falling, yanking at my hands to try to reach out and catch myself, legs flailing, a scream tearing from my throat.

My head bounces on the bush, but just as I expect to topple completely down, my feet come to an abrupt halt.

I look up. I'm half out of the window, and Finn has my shins tucked under one arm like I'm a very tedious carrier bag.

"Millie," he sighs, and drags me back into the room by my feet.

This is the most humiliating moment of my life. I'm going to vomit.

"Do I need to put a bell on you, pet?" he grumbles.

"Only if you want to hear me coming."

"I do, yes," he sniggers, and I realise what I just said.

"Not like that!" My cheeks heat to the temperature of the molten sun. I'm an idiot.

"Mmmhmm." He loops one strong arm around my

shoulders, and the other shifts to beneath my knees and he picks me up like I weigh nothing at all.

I gasp as my side is pressed to him from hip to chest, and my hands are useless, still tethered at the small of my back.

He's hard. Everywhere. His body is utterly solid. I can feel the planes of his muscles, like he's a warm, living marble statue.

"If you wanted to be carried, you should have just said so." He carries me out of the lounge and those green eyes are steady on my face the whole time, mesmerising as being lost in a forest.

Did I want that?

His body against mine again?

"No."

Wow. Very convincing. Finn clearly thinks so too, as he tilts his head to the side and nods sarcastically.

The enclosed stairway puts his face into shadow, and there's a slide of his muscles against my curves as he mounts the stairs.

"Or would you prefer to be spanked?"

I'm speechless.

"I..."

The hand on my legs thumps onto my thigh before I can complete that thought and I squawk.

That... wasn't bad? It kinda tingles pleasantly.

"Behave, or there will be more like that," he warns, and a tremor goes down my spine. Not exactly a bad feeling, either.

He takes me to the bedroom with a double bed and places me down on it, sliding me down his body until my toes touch the floor.

He steps backwards, and shrugs off his suit jacket. For a

moment, I don't understand. Then he flicks open the second button of his green shirt.

We're in a *bedroom*.

Blood rushes in my ears as button by button he reveals first the rest of his chunky, masculine silver necklaces and that dip between his collarbones that makes my mouth water, then a smattering of dark hair, and sculpted muscles that are decorated with black ink in geometric lines. Celtic knots?

He's utterly calm as he pinches his cuffs and shrugs out of the shirt. But me? I'm blushing, and unable to look away.

Because my god, he's the most beautiful thing—human, natural, or object—I've ever seen in my life. He has that V at his hips, a six pack that invites my touch, and a trail of dark hair that leads down further.

I let out a squeak as his hands go to his black leather belt with a shiny metal buckle.

"What are you doing?"

"Don't you know?" he says darkly.

I gulp. I do. And I wish I could say it was the honey with the waffles that made my mouth dry.

Punishing me.

He's so tall, I have to crane my neck to look up at him from where I'm sitting. He has kissable lips. The sort of plush but understated lips that are the envy of any girl who has examined herself critically in the mirror. Though the short black beard that covers his hard jaw, and a nose that has been broken once or twice dispels any hint of softness.

The scars.

I want to ask what he intends, but my brain is unable to think over the clamour of my heartbeat. And also—it's obvious. He told me he'd have compensation from me of a non-monetary kind, and this is it.

I'm at his mercy. I can't stop this big, powerful man from using me however he likes.

And far from panic racing through my veins, it's excitement. I'd never be able to say this aloud, but I want Finn to *take*. There's a peace settling over me that's unlike anything I've ever felt.

"Stand up," he rumbles, and it's the sound of a boulder rolling downhill and about to squash you. He has his trousers half open, and there's a prominent bulge.

A really big one. Intimidating. Terrifying.

I'm shaking. Fear? Excitement? I can't tell.

"Turn around."

But without my volition, I slowly spin until I'm facing the headboard of the bed and staring out of the little four paned window that looks out to the sea.

I think he's going to... Well. I can't do anything to stop him, can I?

Do I even want to?

I hide that thought in the back of my mind.

There's a click. My arm shifts.

For a second I don't know what it means.

Then my other wrist is released.

My head jerks to look over my shoulder—and up—into my captor's face. My face heats with two realisations at the same time, and my cheeks heat.

He will have seen my plain cotton underwear when he looked in the bags. Sensible knickers. Maybe that's why he didn't do what his eyes promised.

And I'm disappointed. I'm absolutely gutted.

I was *looking forward* to that.

"I'll escape, you know." I try to cover how my bravado has sunk without trace. "I'll run."

"I hope you will. *After* we've had a rest. It's been a

long night, pet," he replies with exaggerated patience. "What's happening now is you and I are getting some shut-eye. I was undressing to go to bed. You don't expect me to sleep in these clothes after a night in the car in them, do you?"

"I thought you were going to..." I close my eyes in absolute humiliation and bow my head.

He grabs my neck, and my eyes fly open as he uses his thumb to force my chin back up and turn me around towards him.

"Not until you beg for it."

Adrenaline pulses through me anew, bright and sparkling.

"I want you to plead with me to fuck your mouth. I want your little pink cunt getting all wet and juicy as I shove my cock down your throat," he continues roughly.

It is. The space between my legs is heating as he says that.

"And you're not going to run away, because I'll cuff you again when you've finished changing into something to sleep in."

He withdraws his hand with a caress of my skin, and I'm panting by the time his fingertips leave my chin. Jerking his head towards the door, I take the hint.

I'm in a daze when he sits on the bed, his back to me. There's no chance of escape, and no way to call anyone, since Finn has my phone. So, I do the only logical thing. I put on the pyjamas from my bag and give my teeth a quick brush, and when I'm done, he's waiting.

"Hands," he states and it's not a request.

I present them in front of me, and watch his muscles flex as he snaps the pink fluffy monstrosities onto me with practised ease.

"Do I need to tie your feet while we sleep, or are you going to be a good girl?"

Finn's good girl? Tingles shimmer over my skin. "I'll be good."

"You will, yeah?" He shoots me a wry look, and points at the bed.

"See, I am a good captive." I demonstrate by getting onto the bed and wriggling under the covers.

Finn tugs the curtains closed on all the windows, blocking out a nominal amount of light.

Then he lies down behind me, wraps his arm around my waist and all the air gets expelled from my lungs as he jerks me flush to his chest. He throws one leg over mine, but I notice that his hips are angled away, so I can't feel what I nearly saw. Is that because…

"What are you doing?" I ask softly. "I thought…"

"Go to sleep, Millie." His reply is gruff.

I close my eyes, and despite everything, the warmth of his body and the sensation of being secure—trapped, yes, but I can't do anything about it, and this isn't my fault or my responsibility to sort out for once—has my body relaxing.

I might have accidentally kidnapped Finn, but I'm his captive.

The playboy kingpin wants to keep me. For now.

There's cold at my back when I wake. For a second, the weight of dread sinks into me that my brother is a gambling addict who has put himself in debt way over his head, I'm a nurse whose next shift probably starts in about five minutes, and I'll have hundreds of people to take care of for twelve hours, and I'm alone.

Then I open my eyes, see the cottage bedroom, and I remember the kidnap.

And Finn.

I jolt upright with all the grace of a three-legged panda falling off a log, since my hands are still cuffed. In *pink* fluffy handcuffs.

Ohhh kill me now.

Finn is sprawled in the comfy chair, facing the bed, on his phone. He's changed into a T-shirt and a pair of jeans from my brother's bag, and they're a smidge too small. The white T-shirt picks up threads of grey at his temples that were almost invisible before, and hugs his biceps, revealing the shadows of his tattoos beneath. His brows are low.

I suppose I should be fist pumping because technically I slept with a stunningly *gorgeous man*.

But the cuffs make it difficult, plus he didn't touch me. He was a gentleman, disappointingly. Is the only way I can get a man to spend time with me by deprivation of liberty?

What a fail. I've always been shy and awkward with boys, but this is absurd.

He's beautiful. Powerful. Rich. All the things I'm not, and suddenly I'm really aware of how pointless it is to make this into something it isn't. He's just playing a game with me, like a sleek jungle cat. For all he's wearing casual clothes, he's a jaguar with black fur and green eyes.

Am I seriously thirsting over my victim/captor, when my brother could be in trouble for all I know? Ugh. I'd like to think he'll have been calling me, but I doubt it. We were so close when we were kids, and then long shifts and his gambling "hobby" pushed us apart, leaving me alone.

He is still my little brother. However tall he gets, I'm still the one who made him breakfast cereal when our parents left us for days on end.

"Can you phone my brother? Or can I call him from your phone?" I ask.

Finn looks up, and his expression instantly brightens as his green eyes meet mine.

Then he blinks, as though he has only just processed what I said. "He's a big boy."

There's something evasive in the kingpin's answer, but I can't identify what it might be beyond the obvious. Finn Kilburn likes to be in control.

My gut turns over. While Noah won't even realise I'm gone, I'll be stuck with the man I've been having inappropriate thoughts about, who is probably just toying with the little girl—compared to him—who accidentally kidnapped him.

"He'll be okay without you for a week," Finn continues.

What? Does he not intend to leave immediately after getting some rest?

I can't. I just can't do this.

A week with my crush is humiliation in seven twenty-four-hour shifts on top of whatever punishment Finn has planned. Even dealing with my brother would have been better than falling further for a man who is so out of my league he's like a professional football player and I'm a toddler with a foam ball.

"You don't want to spend that long here." That sounds desperate.

"Don't I?" He puts his phone aside. "Nice house. Beach location. Good company."

"We're strangers!" But already he doesn't feel like a stranger. There's a tug at my heart. I admire this man, despite everything.

"Are we?" he asks softly, narrowing his eyes.

"Aren't we?" Because that's the other thing. The way

he feels familiar and like I've seen his face constantly since bumping into him at Noah's work. I've told myself over and over I'm deluded. Finn isn't everywhere, even in his territory of Kilburn. He's not in the hospital, on the street as I walk to work, or in the queue at the coffee shop.

He's not. That's absurd.

"We've met before," he points out calmly. "Last week."

"Yes, but..." I can't say what I mean here. *Yes, but my tummy goes all squiggly near you, and I have daydreams about you.*

He stares at me, head tilted arrogantly up, as though daring me to admit that I've seen him since then.

"I can get you home," I finish instead.

"I'm not interested in going home. I want *compensation*. And I've decided it will be a week here, with you."

I press my lips together.

Finn stands and paces towards me. I resist the urge to shrink back, but fear judders down my arms and legs. That intense expression in his green eyes indicates the mafia boss is going to exact revenge for my mishap.

He's going to *take everything*.

He might... My mind won't even think of the word.

And yet, heat twists low in my stomach.

"I want something money can't buy," he says, his voice like black silk.

My clit throbs.

He drops one knee between my feet, then leans down over me. I shrink back, lying down. Finn follows, and his breath is warm on my lips, sending a shiver of heated fear and arousal down my spine.

This is crazy. I'm scared, and tied up, and yet...

"Will you let me go if I do what you ask?" I look

between his eyes and his mouth, the excitement stealing all the oxygen in the room.

This isn't the way I thought I'd lose my V-card.

But, honestly, I just haven't imagined losing it. I've never met anyone who made me feel like I wanted to touch them, or to have them touch me.

Until Finn.

There's a pause, and it's probably my imagination, but is his sigh a bit disappointed, his expression weary?

"One week," he says gruffly. "Then we'll return to London. I'll drop you home myself."

He reaches down and snags my pyjama top. I don't breathe as he pulls it oh-so-slowly up. "Seven days, Millie. Until we go back to Kilburn, you're my captive."

As he stares hungrily at my bared breasts, my nipples pucker. The kingpin who made me feel special with a glance makes my skin flush hot.

He's a playboy. That's why he's so good at this. He'll leave me as soon as he's had his fun.

And yet, even knowing all that, I can't help but want him.

7

FINN

She goes rigid and she's shivering with fear, and feck, I'm a bad man, but it gives me a thrill that she's afraid of me. Of what I might do.

Frankly, she's right. I'm not fully in control of myself, I want her that much. I should withdraw, but the way she quakes under me is intoxicating.

I can't help it. I rock against her. Just a bit, a deniable movement. Sordid and wrong and... she rolls her hips. Her neck has gone pink.

A certainty sweeps down my spine.

"Do you like being scared?"

She gasps. "No?"

"Honestly?" I croon. Taking my hand to her face, she doesn't flinch when I stroke her cheek, then down her jaw, and to her neck. Her skin is so soft. She tilts her head up, like a stray cat warily accepting a kind stroke from her new owner.

She doesn't reply.

"If I reach between your legs, you won't be wet and puffy with need, your little clit begging for my touch?"

She mews and pushes up against me, rubbing her core against my length.

The sensation makes my brain stutter, even through multiple layers of fabric and dry cotton boxers. The head of my cock is throbbing.

"Go on, tell me. Whisper to me. Tell me you're not soaking through your knickers," I urge her, grinding my hips down.

I lower my head and position my ear above her lips. She's not really trapped. If she wanted to roll over and wriggle away, she could. I'd let her. Reluctantly.

But I think she doesn't want to get away.

"No," she breathes.

I shift so I can look into her eyes. They're clear and blue and innocent, shining. I search them for an indication she doesn't want this, and find none.

"Liar," I say back, equally soft. "Are you going to scream if I find out?" I creep my hand down, sliding into her pyjama bottoms, and we both gasp as my fingertips touch her knickers.

She goes rigid, and I pause.

A whine of discontent escapes her throat, and I don't know if it's because I stopped, or because of where my hand was going.

"I'd better swallow that scream, huh?" I tease as I lower my mouth to hers, covering hers. "Don't want anyone to hear and find you."

There's no one around. No one to hear if she cried out, or interrupt us from our kinky, forbidden game. This is just a ruse to kiss her. I admit that to myself, even if I can't to her, hiding that this means so much to me. It might just be a kiss, but it's our first kiss, and it's magic. Sparks and rainbows and stupid hearts.

Stupid, stupid hearts, because I've kissed many women —none recently—and never had a kiss like this.

My heart skips from just pressing our lips together. It's so sweet and tender, not at all reflecting the depraved things I want to do to her. I guess the slide of my lips on hers is an apology. The little nibbles and teases are a seduction and a promise.

And a plea. *Trust me. I won't hurt you.*

Except in the ways you'll love.

I love you.

Feck. That's why this is so new. I love her. I've fallen absolutely in love with a girl too young for me, and who fears me.

Grand. Just grand.

It takes soft kisses, patience, and telling her all the ways I love her, for her to relax beneath me.

"Now," I say against her lips. "Should I check, little liar?"

I slide my hand down her body and beneath her waistband again, and this time, when she squeaks with fear, I don't stop. No hesitation. She doesn't move away, only towards, arching up to me. And when my fingertips reach her seam, it's warm and slick. Pouring from her.

Mine-mine-mine-mine.

I knew it. The chant repeats in my head. She's *mine*.

"You're soaking, pet," I say as I withdraw my hand.

"I'm not!" It's as guilty a denial as a kid with chocolate around their face, and I suppress a laugh, as I rear up.

"That wet little cunt of yours says differently."

She's laid on the bed legs apart, looking up at me with embarrassment, and worry, and trust. Her cuffed hands are clasped together at her waist, knuckles white. Something about her pyjamas and that pose, and her little fingers makes me hesitate. She's so young.

"I'm a filthy bastard almost twice your age, who wants to defile you," I confess. "Stop me. Now. Before I can't stop myself. Roll away. Kick me." The words are gravel in my throat.

She doesn't move, only swallowing. Her cheeks are flushed.

"You should stop me, right now." My heart is a lead weight, swinging in my chest.

"No," she whispers, and that's enough.

"Lift your hips," I demand fiercely, reaching for her.

She obeys, and I drag the pyjama bottoms from her, revealing plain white cotton knickers, then the smooth skin of her long legs. Including freckles. They're perfect seasoning over her mouthwatering curves.

I lose my voice. I lose my mind. I can only look at her as I toss away the pyjamas, unthinking, as though I have never seen a woman's legs before. But there's something about the triangle of fabric over her hips that fills me with a hunger more savage than I know what to do with.

My hands are at the waistband of those innocent knickers before I can think better of it, and I don't even have to ask her this time. She arches up, allowing me to draw them down.

Then she's bare and although it's not much that's revealed with the way her knees are modestly together, her squirming beneath my gaze makes my cock jerk in response. The sheer sexiness of this girl might kill me if I don't get my mouth on her and my cock in her immediately.

"Open your legs," I order, my voice even more smoky and dark than usual.

She pants.

"Now," I bite out when she doesn't obey.

"I'm..."

I raise one eyebrow and wait.

She swallows. "I'm..."

There are a number of intriguing ways she could finish that sentence, and I'm curious.

"I've never..."

"What have you never done, pet?" I ask, not daring to hope.

She scrunches her eyes closed then says in a rush, "I'm a virgin."

Jesus Mary and Joseph.

I didn't think I could be any harder, but sure. That'll do it. She's going to be mine to claim in every way. I get to teach her about sex, and ensure that her first is as special and loving as she deserves, and savour each new experience, step by step.

"What about other things?"

"Nothing." She raises her trapped hands to cover her face. "I haven't done anything, alright?"

I take this opportunity to grin from ear to ear. We get to discover all her pleasures together.

"Look at me."

This time she obeys immediately, slowly lowering her arms and revealing a scared and embarrassed little face.

"This is going to be new for me too, pet."

Her eyebrows pinch. "What do you mean?"

"I mean, this is new to me too. I've never..." I hesitate. It's on the tip of my tongue. I could say it now. I've never responded like this. I've never loved a woman before. I've never been this obsessed. I've never had sex without a condom, but when we get that far, there's no way I'm gloving up. I'm going in raw, and breeding her.

Not yet. I want her to beg me for my cock. But I do have to taste her, and that can't wait. Even if the ache in my balls demands I take advantage of her.

"I've never been abducted." She winces, but I continue. "Held a girl prisoner, taught anyone about sex, or been with a woman this much younger than me."

That's less scary for both of us.

"Oh." Is that relief on her face? Was she worried that I might have done this with someone else?

"My special kidnapper," I reassure her. "Spread your legs for me."

Her knees twitch, as though her body wants to do as I say, but her mind is resisting. I place my hands over her inner thighs.

"Show me my compensation," I murmur as I apply the slightest pressure. It's enough. She slides outwards with my palms, and I hold her gaze.

"Brave little pet, that's it." And she likes that. It's obvious in the way her eyes light up. I wonder if she enjoys being praised?

When she gets to the point that her slit begins to open, I nod. "Good girl."

And yes, those are the right words, because she whimpers.

"Such a good girl for me," I rasp.

"I..." Her cheeks tinge pink. There's moisture leaking from her outer pussy lips and my mouth waters in response.

"Go on." I dig my fingertips into her plump flesh. "Show your captor, your new owner, how wet you are from imagining all the depraved things he's going to do to you, pet."

She lets out a little mewl and edges her thighs further.

I groan as her sex is revealed in all its pink, glistening beauty.

"More. I want it all," I say, because I'm a greedy bastard. And this time I do push on her legs forcing them, so she's fully exposed to me. "Feck, so pretty. So, so pretty."

She's soaking wet, her arousal clear and revealing her like rose petals. Her clit is a sweet little bud just begging for my tongue. My cock is jammed against my flies and aching for me to release it and take up the implicit invitation of her dripping pussy.

But first, there's a more important thing to do. I look back up, into her eyes.

"As part of your punishment for kidnapping me, I'm going to make you scream."

8

MILLIE

My captor. My owner. His *pet*.

I've done everything for myself—and Noah—for so long, the idea of being Finn's pet is humiliatingly appealing. Even with the scratch of knowledge in me that for all his heated words, I'm the latest in an endless line of women for the playboy kingpin.

Special. I mustn't believe that. I bet he says it all the time.

"That's it, my pretty girl."

He lowers his head, and I squeak as I realise he's going to put his face near my pussy.

Finn doesn't stop at my noise of distress. With horror, I see him getting really close, just an inch away with his *mouth*.

"No!"

I feel his exasperated exhale, then his green eyes pin me. "What is, Millie?"

"I haven't washed!" My cheeks heat. He'll be so grossed out now I reminded him.

I bet all the girls he's had before have been fresh out of the shower. I, by contrast, am not. I haven't seen a bath since yesterday morning.

His expression changes from irritated that I stopped him to arrogantly knowing.

"Good," he states. "I don't want to dilute any of your taste. I want it all."

There's no time for horror, or space to get away before he licks all the way up my pussy, making me spasm with the unexpected pleasure. His tongue rolls over my clit and shock sharpens the flare of sensation.

"Fecking delicious." He lets out a growling purr that's all masculine contentment and licks me again, this time sucking the bud into his mouth.

I jerk. I gasp and cry out and tug at the handcuffs.

It's... Oh my god. Stunning.

When eventually he releases my clit, I've forgotten everything. I've no idea why I objected, I can't remember any life before I was in this room with Finn, and my own name is a total mystery.

I'm a quivering jelly of need and hormones.

Then he licks me again. Harder.

Trapped by him, I have no shame. I can't stop him, and the noises Finn is making as he works my clit are feral. Like he's doing this as much for himself as he is for me. He's kissing my pussy as though it's an art form, a vocation.

I feel like a priceless treasure that he's creating. Every touch, every flick of his tongue and swipe of his lips, drives me higher. My nipples are pebbled with need, but the overwhelming pleasure from Finn's mouth is sending pulses of bliss right to my toes.

"I could eat you all day," he says without moving, his

voice muffled. "Perhaps I will. Maybe I'll keep you here and lick you out morning, noon, and night, tied to the bed. I'll feed you waffles and give you orgasm after orgasm until you're crying for mercy and can't take anymore."

Then he redoubles his attack on my clit, and I break. I shudder and choke out Finn's name as I come, the pleasure sweeping me away. It's unlike anything I've ever felt.

No responsibilities. No worries. Just Finn feeding me sinfully sweet waffles and making me come. Ugh.

Being restrained somehow heightens every spike of ecstasy, and Finn's mouth is on me throughout. He's controlling it, pushing up the wave and making it bigger and more intense.

Then it's too much, and I must cry out and try to get away, because his hands clamp down on my thighs, but his lips move off my clit, his tongue pushing into my entrance. That only prolongs the tail of the pleasure, until I'm not coming anymore but my god, it's still so good.

He's changed to fucking me with his tongue in firm thrusts that are deeper than I'd think possible with what is undeniably not a big body part. But then, Finn is huge all over, so I guess it's not a surprise that his tongue is penetrating me.

And the vulnerability is unbearably erotic. I'm almost naked, with my pyjama top pushed up and he's clothed, but he's got his head between my legs, and he seems to have no intention of looking up any time soon.

Because he's shifting, continuing to thrust into me, but also slipping upwards, a fraction further each time. Instinctively I try to move away to keep him from my now-sensitive clit, but he doesn't let me. Until he touches it, and then he's covering my clit entirely on every stroke.

It's too much, but it's also not, and he builds my arousal

until I'm gasping and pulling at the cuffs as he's circling my clit with his tongue again.

He releases my thigh, and I don't have time to process what that means, beyond disappointment that he isn't touching me as much, before there's a nudge at my entrance.

I stiffen, even as his tongue on my clit doesn't relent.

"Finn..."

"I know," he says gently, then his finger is sinking in, stretching me to him. I'm malleable in his hands, and so out of control I should be panicking. Perhaps a small part of my mind is still shouting that I shouldn't be allowed to give this up. I should be fighting, or embarrassed. But there's no space for either, because Finn is doing this to me, and in the secrecy of my own mind, I can admit it feels *so good*.

Then everything is overwhelming. His fingers, the sound of him rumbling his approval, the filthy wet squelching sounds of my wetness, and me gasping and sighing.

"Come for me," he says, then redoubles the intensity of his finger inside me, stroking and coaxing me, rubbing on my inner wall. And his tongue is relentless.

"Again."

"I can't, I can't," I babble. My body spirals upwards, obeying him even though I know it's impossible. I can't do it with my fingers, I've tried.

"One more for me, pet." His voice is decadent and tempting. He's pure sin.

"I..." It feels good, but there's a sharp edge to the pleasure that has always made me back off. With Finn, I'm embracing it.

"You can." His confidence is so sexy it sends a bolt of need through me. Then he's silent as his mouth returns to my core, gentle but somehow knowing my body better than I do myself.

"It hurts, please, it hurts." And that's true, and it seems like a plea for him to stop. I tell myself that's what it is. But I'm arching up into him, towards the pain and the pleasure, not away.

"Do it for me." And his request sounds heartfelt, like it would be a favour to him if I allowed him to make me orgasm. He shifts his focus from my clit and for a second I think he's going to let me off, but he doesn't. It's an adjustment, and instead of licking right over the nub, he's running his tongue around the base, and I almost levitate.

Combined with his fingers, and the earthy scent of his skin, and the low noises of contentment he's making, I'm helpless.

I break apart in a jagged orgasm unlike anything I've felt before. It's unfamiliar, and shocking in its force. It shakes me, but Finn holds me firm, stable as granite cliffs against the sea, and I toss and writhe as the white-hot sparks shower down every limb.

I'm panting when I can think again. My cheeks are heated, my pussy is tingling with aftershocks, and when I look between my legs, Finn is pressing lazy kisses to the insides of my thighs, his green eyes flashing up at me, full of a serious emotion I can't interpret.

Then he smacks my soaking folds lightly, as though to say, *Don't worry, I'll be back for more*, and levers himself up and over me.

I shudder. It's possessive, that smack. A promise.

This is what people mean when they say Finn is charming but ruthless. He kills with a smile, and tortures with orgasms. A flirt, I remind myself, but I can't find the energy to care.

He shoves his jeans down and pulls out his cock. I gasp. A vein runs down the length, and liquid beads at the tip, and it's almost red it's so swollen. Is that painful?

Then he grips it, and a tremor goes through me. He's not going to... Is he?

I'm helpless. At his mercy.

9

FINN

She stares at my cock, eyes wide.

"You like the look of this, huh?" Swiping my hand over my length, the pleasure streaks down my spine. I won't last long. She's too beautiful.

I lean forward, and panic flashes over her face.

"Are you going to..."

"Shove my fat cock into your mouth and make you take it as I fuck your throat?" I finish for her.

She lets out a squeal of alarm.

"Fuck that tempting little pussy of yours?"

A full, head-to-toe tremble shakes her. But she doesn't shy away.

"You have no idea how much I want to accept that offer, pet." But I can't risk scaring her off, and I have a different claim in mind for right now.

Licking her lips, her expression nearly breaks my resolve.

But I hold out my hand in front of her mouth, not quite touching.

"Spit," I demand simply.

"What are you...?" she whimpers.

Deliberately, teasingly, I lower my hips, so the heated length of my cock brushes on her inner thigh. I can't contain a groan as the head touches her wetness—both from my tongue and the cream of her arousal. It takes all my control to hold myself there, and not thrust into her warm, tight pussy.

"Unless you want me to take lubrication from a different part of your body," I rumble, and in my imagination, I rut myself over her already over-sensitised clit, rocking out another climax from her.

I half want her to refuse so I can have the excuse.

She lets out a whimper, and she closes her eyes. "I can't spit. It's so dirty."

Ah, but this is more fun.

"Now." My tone brooks no argument.

She opens her eyes again and they're sparkling with disbelief.

"I..."

"I can't wait any longer, pet." I shift against her entrance, just the slightest bit.

Her lips pout, and the seconds draw out.

Then she hawk-tuhs onto my palm with the enthusiasm of the perfect little slut she is.

I close my fingers over her saliva, relishing this small piece of her.

"Good girl." I lift my hips away from her sweet pussy and bring my hand to my cock. I groan as my wet fingers slide over the throbbing helmet. Bliss.

And despite having just come—repeatedly—Millie's eyes are bright with desire as her gaze dips to where I'm beginning to stroke myself then back to my face.

"I love you watching me like that," I confess as my fingers tighten, my forearm tensing.

She licks her lips, her little pink tongue unconsciously arousing.

"So sexy." But I'm not even looking at the obvious parts of her as I jerk my cock fast and rough with her spit. Nope. I looked plenty at her arse—admittedly via cameras, and with clothes on—but her tits and her nipped waist and *every part of her* is gorgeous. But the thing that got me hard as stone was licking her out, and the sight that will tip me over is Millie watching me.

It's the revelation of her desire that turns me on, when I thought I might be suffering on my own here.

"You are amazing."

My balls draw upwards, and pleasure coils. I'm going at this vigorously, with all the pent-up lust of not having her when I *need* her.

"Finn," she breathes.

I blow.

That one word—my name on her plush, pink lips and from her hot mouth—has my orgasm barrelling up and spurting out in waves of ecstasy.

"Millie." My answering groan is choked as I stroke myself through wave after wave. I cover her belly, a possessive, primal claim. "Mine," I grunt out, as a final surge hits me unexpectedly.

I'm wrecked by the intensity of coming in her presence, not just watching her from afar. I can't stop looking at her. Half naked, legs spread, and covered in the slick, shiny evidence of her desire and mine.

Straightening the arm I'm holding myself on, I take filthy delight in having marked her with ropes of white.

Owning her. I'd make them into fecking tattoos if I

could, except that stretch marks from having my baby will do that perfectly.

My hand shakes as I scoop up my semen from her soft belly and draw it down as she looks on in disbelief. I smear it over her mons then part her pussy lips.

She winces as I run my fingers around her clit, not over it, but near. Just close enough to threaten.

"Too sensitive?" I tease.

"Mmm!" she whimpers, nodding desperately.

"Spread your legs wider for me so I can push this seed where it belongs." I slide my fingertips down and put the smallest amount of pressure on her entrance, nudging at it to tell her what I mean.

A shudder goes through her from head to toe, and she obeys, reopening for me where her knees had fallen inwards.

Slow but relentless, I sink two fingers into her.

"So hot, and still dripping wet for me," I observe, trying to be objective, but not managing in the least. "You'll feel like heaven when this is my cock."

"Don't..." she whispers.

I continue, one knuckle, the next, then pressing into the base of my hand and pulling my fingertips upwards to caress her inner walls. She moans.

"I could get you pregnant like this, my little virgin pet," I croon as she arches onto my fingers. She's not trying to run away. "You're so beautiful it's almost a pity to defile you with my cock. I could breed you like this and watch you come apart for me over and over."

She makes an incoherent noise, then squeaks as I swipe my thumb over her clit. "You don't mean that."

"No," I agree. "I need more for my compensation for being kidnapped." I draw back my fingers then shove them back in. "I want to fuck you hard." Again. "With my fingers." Another thrust. "My tongue. My cock. Every. Fecking. Thing. I own. I want in. Your. Soaked. Pussy."

"Why?" she gasps out.

I think she's close to coming again.

"Because I want your scent over everything," I tell her, but she's moaning so much I don't think she hears. "I want you in my life, unerasable."

I smile as she breaks, tensing and sobbing as she comes again from my touch. It's the hottest experience I've ever had, because this time, it's with my seed inside her.

Her pussy squeezes my fingers so hard I'm certain for a moment that she'll cut off my bloody circulation, or maybe devour my fingers entirely. Then it recedes like a tide, until her body goes from taut to almost liquid.

Her eyes are closed, and I examine her at my leisure, leaving my fingers as a pacifier in her warm, ravenous little cunt.

"You're so responsive," I tell her. She's mind-blowing. She's going to come on my cock so beautifully.

After a couple of minutes, a cramp sets into my shoulder.

I ignore it. Part of the price of being a filthy bastard who is twice the age of this perfect angel under me is that I should feel the discomfort of my body not being twenty anymore.

She's so good and sweet, and three orgasms have knocked her out.

Then my knee begins to ache, and I admit defeat.

"Have I killed you?" I ask, teasingly, and reluctantly slide my fingers from the bliss of her wet passage.

Her eyelids flutter.

In the seconds it takes to find the key and unlock the

cuffs, she's stirred, and her big blue eyes are watching me. I gather her into my arms, and she wraps her legs around my waist.

And the second her naked breasts touch my chest, I know for sure. I thought it was true before, but I had no idea. The trusting way she snuggles into me as I carry her to the bathroom solidifies every bone-deep instinct I've had about Millie.

I'm never letting her go.

10

MILLIE

"Such a good girl," he murmurs, over and over, as he washes me in the shower that absolutely doesn't have room for two. It's one of those square cubicles and doesn't even have room for one of Finn. But he manoeuvred us in together like a stunt driver handbrake parallel parking into a space with an inch at each end, and manages to keep the shower head on me—at the perfect temperature—the whole time.

Being squashed in somehow emphasises how big he is, and it makes me feel tiny, and sheltered. And near him.

I've never felt this close to anyone.

I guess I've never been with another person in this way. In bed. In the bathroom. Taking a shower together feels just as exposing as spreading my legs and having him lick me until I totally lost control of my body. It seems I gave it all up to *him*. And when he gets a glint in his green eyes as he rubs a soapy palm over my breast, I can't think of any reason not to continue to let him have anything he wants.

Not because I kidnapped him, and then he kidnapped me, or whatever convoluted thing is going on here, but because being with him feels so perfect. Better than I've felt for...ever.

I'm not in cuffs, but there's no way I can run. I'm weak.

He takes my hand and lifts my arm, and we're palm to palm. My heartbeat kicks up again at the size difference between us. Then he curls his fingers over the tips of mine and his blunt square nails reach almost to my second knuckle.

It's too much.

I squeeze my eyes tightly shut.

I've had to be in control and manage everything for so long, and now Finn has taken command entirely. Even to the extent of washing me.

Emotions I've tried to keep down bubble up. Things like, I'm so tired. This is the first time I've felt cared for since... I can't remember. I wish someone looked after me like this forever. Finn. I long for Finn to really care for me.

I want to be special to him, for real.

But I kidnapped the playboy kingpin. A billionaire almost twice my age, who could have anyone he wanted. I'm a novelty right now, but it'll wear off, just as the amusement of having children wore off for my parents.

11

FINN

I wrap her in a fluffy towel, and I'm a terrible person, because I can't keep away, so I use the two ends to trap her, draw her towards me and kiss her mouth. A tender kiss that doesn't reveal how I crave her again, but more this time. I need her complete surrender.

Back in the bedroom, we both dress silently, and it's only when we're both fully clothed—she's in a pair of cut-off jean shorts and a T-shirt that I instantly want to remove—that I approach her with the cuffs. She sighs and offers me her hands.

A sense of peace descends on me as I secure them to her wrists. She can't escape me.

"What do we do now?" she asks as she tests the cuffs.

"This is your party," I point out. "You brought me here."

She huffs. "You aren't the guest I was expecting."

"Less related and less addicted," I agree. "Isn't that a good thing? What were you going to do with Noah?"

"I had a load of therapy things for addicts planned. Walks, food, reflective questions, and exercises. That sort of stuff."

She looks sad, and that sounds like a lot of work that she put into this. My sweet pet. She didn't know I had it all in hand for her. The update on Noah I got this morning is that he's being open to the first stages of the process. Admittedly, he has the threat that I'll kill him if he doesn't get his act together. And he's unaware it's an empty threat, because he isn't aware that I'm in love with his sister, and would rather gnaw off my own arm than upset her.

"Will you show me?" I say gently.

She sighs, and gestures with her chin to her bag. "It's all in a folder."

"Go on then." I'm not going through her stuff again. That way lies madness.

It takes her a moment to get a blue document wallet with her hands tethered, and she brings it to me, then rolls her eyes when I don't take it.

"Finn. What am I supposed to do? Hold it with my teeth?"

"Your mouth should be put to better use," I mutter, but I can't help but smile. I grab the key from my pocket and undo the cuff on her left hand.

"What are you doing?"

I snap the cuff over my left hand and Millie's eyes widen in surprise.

"Giving you use of one hand, but preventing you from escaping." Keeping her close, more importantly. I tug her with me and lead her downstairs to the lounge. Away from the temptation of the bed.

I pull her onto the sofa by our linked wrists, but she resists, sitting bolt upright where I would prefer she was closer to me.

"Is that comfortable?"

"Yes."

Sighing, I ease back onto the cushions.

"Don't lie to me, Millie." I tug on her wrist, and because she's so on edge, it unbalances her immediately. I take the advantage, and lift my arm over her head as she falls, bringing her to rest in the crook of my armpit against my chest.

She gasps, but my arm is resting over her belly now, keeping her to me when I think she'd otherwise wriggle up. Then she exhales and sinks into me.

"See, that's better."

I look at the notebook again. It's bursting with printouts and covered with bookish stickers, including one that says, "Came for the Plot".

"The plot, eh," I comment as I flick it open.

"I like books," she mutters.

The first paper has an addiction recovery plan, with steps. The next is a different version. Then there are pages and pages of detailed notes.

"You did all this, for your brother?" There are days of research and work in this notebook.

Her lip trembles, and when she nods, I know it's because she doesn't trust her voice.

"He's very lucky to have you."

It falls open on a page that has most of the paper stuffed in, and there is a list headed "Questions to encourage communication from addicts" in cutely rounded handwriting.

I skim down the notes.

"Tell me about events that led you to where you are," I read aloud.

"It was dark," she replies promptly. "I couldn't see, and I thought you were my brother."

"Mmm. I'll let you get away with that excuse for now." But before the week is up, she's going to admit that she knew she didn't have her brother. Aside from anything else, he's a good two inches shorter than me. "Go on then. Tell me what led you to kidnapping a kingpin."

"Nothing," she replies defensively.

"Yeah, I believe you." I shake my head. "Totally normal reaction. Everyday. Happens four times a month and extra in February."

"There's nothing! I'm normal."

That's true, and yet it's not. "You're twenty-two, right?"

"How do you know that?"

Stalking.

"I know many things, comes with the job." I'm not telling her I've found out everything I can about her. I know her birthday, and her address. I know where she works, and I had one of my men hack into the CCTV so I can watch her. I know where she buys her coffee before her shifts at the hospital, and which books she downloads to read on her phone. Her age is just a filthy little side note. She's too innocent for me, but I can't bring myself to stop.

"You're very young to be taking on your brother's addiction." Or to be a kingpin's obsession.

She shrugs. "I'm the only one."

Indeed. For me, too.

"What about your parents?" I ask, although I know the answer already.

"They're dead, and I can't just let him destroy his life, and mine." She sounds miserable.

"Friends? Or family friends?" I've only been finding out about her for a week. I might have missed something.

She shakes her head. "My parents weren't like that."

"Why didn't you ask someone else to help?" Me. She could have asked me.

"Don't you get it? There's no one." Her voice breaks at the end of the sentence, and her body suddenly feels heavier against my chest, like the weight of her burden of carrying all this responsibility is more present in her than before.

"That sounds very lonely."

She nods jerkily. Reluctant and proud, even now.

"You've had to be so strong." I stroke her hair. "Dealing with this on your own. Bet it was hard."

She gives a little squeak, as though she's trying to say yes, but can't fully get the word out.

"You've done so well." I tighten my fingers, making her feel my hold on her, in a wordless message of "I've got you. You're safe."

She curls into me, and I absorb it all. Her disappointment in her brother and her parents, all her loneliness. I keep stroking her hair and neck.

The act of being what she needs soothes me in a way I hadn't expected. I like being her pillow as she lets out all the tension she's been holding.

"Want to tell me about it?" I prompt. My cuffed hand creeps over hers and our fingers gradually interlace. No doubt she hasn't noticed, but I'm aware of every fractional shift that leads to my big paw to be linked with her dainty, vulnerable little hand.

"There's not much to tell," she says between sniffs.

"When did you start looking after Noah?"

She shrugs. "I always have."

The story comes out in patches and my heart breaks for the small girl that she was, taking on all the responsibilities of an adult. *That's what big sisters were for*, she was told, and she still obviously believes that, even as she reveals how her parents were neglectful. How she had to fend for herself and her younger brother time after time. The occasion they were left home alone for two weeks at Christmas when Millie was eleven and Noah nine, and Millie couldn't figure out how to use the oven, so they had cereal and sandwiches leaves me biting back that it's a good thing they're dead, otherwise I'd kill them myself.

"Cold food still makes me sick," she jokes, and bile rises in my throat. I'll cook for her every day. She'll never eat anything cold with me.

They used Millie as an unpaid carer for her younger brother, and then, to cap it all, died in a plane crash when she was eighteen and about to leave for university and she was left as her brother's guardian.

Resting fully on me now, she takes a deep, contented sigh and shifts. Her free hand touches my forearm. For a second it's just accidental. Then it's not. She's stroking my arm hair, and tracing the pattern of my tattoos beneath.

"So you see, there's only Noah and me," she says, petting my forearm like it's her emotional support animal. I think she might have forgotten it's attached to me at all. Not a problem. I can be that for her. "And that's why I need to return to London. I fucked up my little 'intervention'."

"You should have asked for help from me, pet."

She huffs sceptically.

"Go on. Ask now," I say gently.

"I already have. I've offered to take you back to London and you refused because you want compensation."

"Ask me why it was me who walked out of the back door of the pub that night, when you expected your brother?"

Her hand pauses on my arm, and she twists so she can look into my face.

"Why didn't my brother come out from the pub?" she echoes tentatively, eying me as though she's about to step off a cliff and she's not sure I've made her wings strong enough.

"He's at my house," I reply simply. "With a gambling addiction therapist, and without his phone, which is why he hasn't messaged you." The outrageously expensive therapist told me firmly that it was too much temptation to have his phone with him.

Her jaw drops open. "But you, I..."

"You think I don't know what is happening with my employees," I say dryly.

"You know about the private lives of all of them?"

"No. Your brother is special."

A bolt of panic crosses her face, and I laugh.

"Not like that. Not for himself, pet. Ask me why I walked out of the pub."

A little crease forms between her eyes, and I reach and smooth it away. She leans into my touch, and I end up with my fingers laced in her hair.

"You came to tell me about Noah?"

I nod. "To invite you to stay with me for the duration of his treatment."

"At your house?"

"At *your* house, as it turned out."

It's some hours after the revelation of Noah being in treatment back in London and I've explained the whole process to her. She's read the updates from the therapist on my phone and discovered everything is as I promised. Afterwards, we watched a movie, with her snuggled in my arms, and had a walk along the beach, her knuckles brushing mine all the way until I gave in and grabbed her hand.

Now we're back at the cottage, in the kitchen as the sun sets outside.

"I can help," she suggested when I paused, wondering how best to do things when cuffed together.

"No," was the simple answer. She doesn't cook anymore. I'm not her brother, for her to look after, or one of her patients. I provide for *her*. And if that sounds caveman-ish? Well, I guess that's why the Irish have a bit of a reputation.

So I rejoined her hands, made her a drink, and set about cooking something hot and delicious for her to eat.

"What about you? What happened that you became the mafia don of Kilburn? Parents dead? Tragic backstory?" she says lightly when she's run out of questions about food.

I catch her eye, and she's trying to appear nonchalant, but the intensity of her sidelong gaze reveals her. She's as curious about me as I am about her.

"Both my parents are alive, and I have six brothers and sisters back in Ireland. My father runs the Cork mafia, so you could say it's the family business."

Her eyebrows shoot up. "But why London?"

"I'm the middle of seven children. No one took any notice of me, I was just the middle boy of the O'Connor family when I was a kid. I think it lit a fire under me to prove myself on my own, so I came to London when I was your age. It took me a few years," and more than a few murders, "but I got control of Kilburn."

"And are you happy with your life?" She reads from the notebook as she plays with a strand of her hair that has come loose from her ponytail and glints in the evening light.

"I thought being on my own would make me happy, since I left because Cork felt too crowded. But I feel like something has been missing, and it wasn't my family back in Ireland. Going to visit them was no help. I didn't realise until very recently what the feeling was. I was lonely."

"But you spend every night in the pubs of Kilburn, laughing, drinking, and..." She blushes and looks away.

"And having women throw themselves at me," I finish for her.

"Mmmhum." Her eyebrows lower fractionally.

"Are you jealous, pet?" I fecking love that idea. Let her be possessive of me. She can be a lioness protecting what's hers.

"Pfft. Don't be ridiculous," she scoffs, but there's something insincere about it.

I grab her chin and force her to meet my eyes. And I was right. She's practically green. "Liar."

Biting her lip, her gaze slides away.

"Pet," I say severely. "Look at me."

She does, and the wobble of concern is so clear in her that my heart aches and lifts simultaneously. "I haven't flirted with anyone since we met. I know I have a reputation as a player," and it's warranted, "but I haven't slept with anyone for almost seven years."

"Really?" she says, scepticism pouring out of her.

"Yes. I was lonely, and I didn't realise why having women didn't fill the gap."

The flicker of hurt and fury is back at the word women, like it's repeating on her. Won't be mentioning that again. I'll never do anything that makes her feel worried that she isn't the whole of my life. My sun, around which everything else spins.

"And in the end, I stopped, because it just made the

ache worse. Spending time with my family, or the men under my command doesn't help either."

"I know what it is to be lonely," she confesses, leaning her head into my palm as I shift to cup her jaw, but it's almost pained. Reluctant. "You don't have to lie to me."

"I have found one thing that makes me feel whole." I dangle the bait before her.

It's her. I'll tell her, if she just asks.

"I'm glad." But she doesn't sound glad. She's gone brittle, and sits up, flicking open her notebook. "Hey, what about this question? 'What would your life be like if you didn't think about your addiction anymore?'"

"Shite." Simple answer. The thought of going back to life before Millie holds about as much appeal as living in an underground bunker the size of a coffin for the next forty years. I can barely breathe at the very idea of how unbearable it would be.

"Ah. Well." Her mouth twists and she shifts position on the sofa. "I think you're supposed to answer that freedom would be better."

"It wouldn't for me. Are you not going to ask me what makes my life complete, pet?"

"It's not gambling is it?" she asks, faux lightly.

"No, but it is an obsession of sorts," I confess hoarsely.

"Oh." She nibbles her lip, and shakes her head, and mutters, "I guess I know. Sex. Women."

Ah feck. I've built my reputation of being a playboy to be bulletproof, and Millie believes it as absolutely as anyone in London. And why do I think she shouldn't? If I said I think I'm in love with her, she wouldn't believe me, and I don't blame her.

"Come on. Hot food for my captive."

She looks up at me, confusion in her expression.

And I smile.

Because I can't tell her, but I can *show* her.

Later, she falls asleep in my arms again.

I stay awake for a long, long time.

I have one week to make her love me, and more importantly, trust that I'm not a player anymore. I'm hers.

12

MILLIE

There is no doubt that I should be hating being a captive, but I don't.

This time, the cuff is around only one of my hands, and it links us together. He's breathing slow and deep behind me, his chest touching my back with every inhale.

Probably this would be a chance to try to escape. The key is in his pocket, and there's a good chance I could get it and lock him up.

Lying in the watery morning light, the scenario plays out in my head. I would feel behind me, reach into the warm pockets of his grey sweatpants, and would my fingers brush the solid weight of his cock? I'd silently undo the cuff, and attach it to the bed. Then I'd leave the warmth of his embrace and the bed, and creep out alone into the cold air. Not stopping for coffee, I'd get into the car, and I'd drive the whole way back to London myself, with no one to talk to or share the trip with.

In my apartment, Noah might not even be there, or maybe he'd be gambling on his phone when I walked in. Perhaps he wouldn't even look up.

The thing is, he'd probably wake up if I reached for the key. Or worse still, he'd think I was trying to touch his cock.

I close my eyes so it's grey instead of brightening sunshine.

Maybe I owe the mafia boss some loyalty, after all, he has helped Noah in a way I couldn't.

I can see why women fall over themselves to be with Finn. Not only is he gorgeous, powerful, filthy rich, and with an edge of danger that makes him even more attractive, he's unexpectedly kind.

The waffles. Dinner last night. Everything he's done for Noah, brushing it off as nothing.

Plus, gotta admit... The orgasms.

What I don't fully understand is why, when he made it clear he was furious I'd brought him here against his will, and he implied he'd have anything he wanted as compensation, he hasn't taken my virginity. After his initial anger, he's been nothing but considerate.

And the shameful truth is, I enjoy having him look after me. I really like there being no choice for me but to do what he says, and I especially love that this cannot be my fault.

I'm not responsible for what he forces me to do.

And his heavy, solid presence behind me and the memory of the way he touched me is delicious. It sends anticipation skittering through me. He makes me feel alive and hot in a way I've never felt before, and never with a man. Tingly.

I close my eyes and think of his face. The scars. I want to know the stories behind them. I want more kisses from his perfectly imperfect lips.

I'm getting achy between my legs, and slick.

This is so wrong. I squirm.

What if I... Take the edge off? If I've already come, I

wouldn't be so susceptible. My heart wouldn't patter whenever he touches me, which is all the time given we're joined by the cuffs.

Maybe then I could say no and mean it, or move away and not towards him.

He didn't take my virginity, but surely he will? And how will I cope, being another notch on his bedpost when he's everything I've ever wanted?

So I edge my cuffed hand down between my legs. The angle is awkward, but it's possible.

The first touch is such relief, I let out a sigh.

Something in the air changes, and I press onto my clit harder.

"Millie," Finn says, huskily, his voice rusty from sleep. "What are you doing?"

"Nothing!" I whisper.

"Are you touching yourself, pet?" He reaches around me, and I freeze, my clit throbbing. He knows. I can't move, but I'm flushing scarlet.

I thought falling out the window was bad? I had no idea.

"Millie..." His breath ghosts my ear, and he pulls me roughly to him, so the hot, hard length of his cock is wedged against my bottom. If I was molten before, now I'm liquid. I'm steam. I've boiled off and become nothing but the places he's touching me.

"If you need to come, all you need to do is *ask*."

13

___

FINN

It took some negotiating with Noah's therapist, but we arranged a daily messaging time, so Millie doesn't worry about her brother. Admittedly, I had to threaten death, but we compromised with life and that they are both monitored for their interactions, albeit for very different reasons.

I watch over Millie so she can't plan an escape, and after a few days she's even getting to check her emails, because the routine of her sitting in my lap and me watching over her shoulder is delicious. I breathe in the apple scent of her hair, nuzzle her neck, and generally indulge myself.

"You're distracting me!" she exclaims when I nip her ear.

"You're taking too long." Even though she uses that tiny keyboard at the speed of light, where I would grumble and make typos and give up after two words. It reminds me how much younger than me she is.

It should feel filthy to have this girl so close, and it does. But it also feels *right*.

The dots are bouncing to indicate Noah is replying to her message. She's asked how his "compulsory training" is going. That's how he refers to it. An imaginative way of describing me surrounding him with my men and telling him if he wanted to keep his job and his life, he would be working sincerely with the gambling counsellor that I've paid an outrageous amount of money for, and not asking too many questions about why.

I was probably a tad forceful, but when I made the connection between Millie running off from the pub and generally looking down as I stalked her, and her brother's expensive hobby, I wasn't in any mood to compromise.

Blowing on her ear makes her giggle, so I do it again.

"Finn!"

"That's plenty of time you've had," I grumble. "Wrap it up."

"I need to know about—"

I grab the phone and toss it away. Within a second I have her top down and her nipple in my mouth and she's moaning. And then we forget about everything else.

"What are you making?" She peers over her mug of tea, sipping it while I'm making dinner. Her hands are in the pink fluffy handcuffs, and she's wearing a cute pink sundress that almost matches.

"Do you like chips?" I indicate the potatoes I'm cutting.

She pinches her eyebrows together. "They're French fries."

They are skinny, I admit, but they'll cook quicker, and I prefer them crispy.

"Are you calling my potato sticks small?" I point the tip of the kitchen knife at her with a wry look.

She puts down her tea and leans forward. The neckline of her dress flops forward and I get a peek at her cleavage.

"Tiny." Her eyes sparkle.

"You shouldn't try to tell an Irishman the correct way to eat potatoes," I growl. But I'm entranced by her. Obsessed. There's no way I can continue with meal prep without risking my fingers being cut off as I'm not paying attention.

"Miniscule." She raises her hands and wiggles one little finger provocatively. "Barely worth eating."

"Is that what you think of the size of my…?" Because if we're talking about my cock, she's very wrong, and we both know it. "Potatoes."

Rising, she slips around the table to where I'm prepping food on the other side, her hips swaying even as her hands are clasped demurely together.

Not an accident, I'm sure.

"Petite." She's goading me.

I keep the knife steady, and she moves until the sharp point touches the dip between her breasts.

"You're being very rude about my cooking, for a woman who has been eagerly eating whatever I offer her." Her tits. My god she's everything. I let the knife rest there, above her beating heart and those plush orbs I want to suck. Then she bites her lip, and that little gesture gets me hard, instantly.

"You aren't giving me anything really satisfying to eat," she replies. "Not big enough."

She's been well fed since we've been here, but I haven't made her give me a blowjob, or had sex with her. They feel like things that need more honesty between us. But maybe the advantage is that she's beginning to *want* my cock in her mouth.

I can work with that.

But she's not getting a treat for being a brat.

"You..." I run the wickedly sharp blade down to her cleavage, fluid and light. Enough to threaten, but not harm. "Need to stop talking."

Her neck flushes pink.

"Make me," she breathes.

Slowly, I take the metal between my thumb and fingers, and turn the knife. Then I raise it, and ease the handle towards her mouth until the smooth, blunt resin edge touches her lip.

"Open up."

Like honey dripping off a spoon, she parts her lips, and I slide the stem in, all the way until it hits the back of her throat. Her breathing goes ragged and her pretty blue eyes remain on my face beautifully.

"See, quiet now, aren't you?" I say, allowing my amusement to seep through.

She makes a needy sound.

"Such a *good girl*." My good girl. "Close your mouth and hold your gag. No dropping it."

I consider leaving her there. Silent, a bit humiliated. Drooling around the knife handle as she watches me make her dinner. But then another idea occurs to me.

"Turn."

She spins, her head not quite steady with the weight of the blade.

"Lean over and rest on the table."

This draws a whimper, but no refusal.

"If you drop the knife, I'll stop," I murmur and sink to my knees behind her. Pushing her skirt up, I groan as I find innocent white cotton knickers. A rumbling purr rises from my chest, and my cock presses against my jeans so hard I think the imprint of the zipper might be permanent.

I slide down her knickers so they're at her bare ankles, then tap her left foot. She lifts it without being asked.

This is insanity. Her hands are tethered, but it wouldn't be difficult for her to get the knife before I realised.

But it's trust, this game. And I'm telling her that I trust and want her.

Even if she's a brat about perfectly good potato foods, and there'll be no fecking nonsense about my choices there.

"Now spread your legs for me, pet," I demand, leaning into where her slick pink folds are exposed. "And stay quiet. If you're going to be rude about the food I'm making you, then I'll eat my dessert first, and you will *wait*."

Millie

"Are the cuffs really necessary?" I ask as he fastens my wrist to his again.

I don't say that I wouldn't run now. Four days, and I don't know why I would. I'm utterly seduced.

"Unless you want to wear a collar and a lead?" Finn replies with a sly smile.

"Finn, I'm not a dog."

"No, you're my pet." He tips my chin up with his thumb and looks down into my eyes. "And I'm not risking you getting away."

Finn

. . .

I scowl at her wrists. They've got some kind of chafing from the cuffs that mars her skin. I find ointment in the bathroom cupboard, and Millie sits obediently as I smooth it over the place where her veins are right at the surface, the blood pulsing through. So beautiful. So vulnerable.

My jaw sets as I realise I should have protected her better.

I pick up the handcuffs.

"Fecking pink fake fur," I grumble.

She can't wear them anymore. Clearly.

"What if I promised not to escape?" she suggests tentatively, and my eyes fly to her face as my heart explodes.

Yes. Of course, yes. That's what I want, for her not to try to leave me.

I draw my eyebrows together. "Touching at all times."

She nods quickly, and for a second I think it's because she's as eager to be close to me as I am to her.

Then I come to my senses.

But still. When I take her little hand in mine and lead her back to the kitchen to put the kettle on for tea, I swear I feel her fingertips press into the tendons on the backs of my scarred knuckles.

14

MILLIE

One day before we're due to go back to London, we're strolling down the beach, his massive paw enveloping mine. This week has begun to feel like an enforced honeymoon. He always shortens his stride to fit mine when we walk along the beach together. It's romantic, if I'm honest.

I've been trying not to think that, and neither of us have talked about tomorrow. During one of my supervised email sessions I saw that someone has offered over the asking price for the cottage, so this really is it.

The cuffs are still off, on the condition that I hold Finn's hand, even though my wrist is fine now. He was overreacting to slight marks made when he accidentally put the cuffs on too tight.

He hasn't taken my virginity, but he takes the touching at all times rule very seriously.

This morning, he tied all four of my limbs to the bed and then licked me with such leisurely patience, bringing me to the brink over and over, that by the time he finally made me come I was a complete mess. He might not want sex, but maybe that's because my mafia boss is as much of a control freak as I am, maybe even more.

Wait.

Mine?

When did that sneak in?

"What are you thinking, pet?" he rumbles, tucking me under his arm. He's freaking huge.

That you're mine. For one more day, and my heart doesn't understand this will be over tomorrow.

"Just that you've been pretty nice."

He barks with laughter.

"For a captor, you know," I add.

"With all your experience of being a captive, that's your judgement?" he teases me, running his thumb up and down my wrist.

"I don't have to have been a captive before to know," I protest.

"Sure, saw it on TV, right?"

"Woman's intuition." I think it's a fair assumption that a mafia boss would be cruel.

He grunts sceptically, a deep noise from the back of his throat and I suddenly remember thinking my brother wasn't talking to me in the car. I seriously thought that was Noah?

"Sometimes you just know," I add. "It's like..." Falling in love.

He's cared for me, listened, and I don't think I've ever had so many days in a row with hot food I didn't cook myself. He's been kinder than anyone I can remember.

Sometimes, you don't have to have seen something before to be certain it's true.

I think I love you.

It's like the first time I came under his tongue. Exhilarating. Unexpected and not what I believed I wanted, but *right*. So right. I guess it's Stockholm syndrome, but now I've found the label, "love", I'm reluctant to give it up.

Love. This is a disaster. I bet a woman falls in love with him every time a butterfly flaps its wings, or whatever the saying is. Every time a mafia don has spaghetti for dinner.

I make an involuntary sound of distress. And of course Finn hears, because he's observant as the big grey wolf he is.

"What is it, pet?" His green eyes sparkle in the warm pre-sunset sunshine as he scans my face, then he scowls and stops us from walking.

"Nothing." Ugh, I'm no good at lying.

I focus on the dip between his collarbones that I want to lick and convince myself this can last forever. Also a lie.

"Sure, yeah," he drawls. "You were fine, and suddenly you went all tense and made a noise like you've been banjaxed."

"I don't know what that means—"

"It means broken," he says urgently. "What is it?"

Should I tell him?

Maybe I should—

Briiinnnnggg.

An obnoxiously loud ringtone shatters the peace of the early evening.

"Ah feck." Finn pulls his phone from his pocket and stares at it.

Squeezing me closer, he mutters, "Sorry, I have to take this, or I suspect our little holiday will come to an abrupt end earlier than planned. Yes?"

"Kilburn, I thought you wanted to remain the London Mafia Syndicate?"

Finn rolls his eyes.

"Look, the first rule of Maths Club—"

Maths Club? I must have misheard. I guess they said mafia club.

"Is that you don't talk about how ridiculous the nickname is?" Finn interrupts.

"Is that you're not supposed to kidnap people," the man finishes without a beat.

A mafia club with no kidnapping. Huh. Rules me out then. That and not being a mafia boss.

Finn laughs. "Ah, yeah. About that."

"I'm sorry if I got you into trouble," I hiss.

"Is that the girl?" the man on the phone demands. "Is she okay?"

"Here, you can speak to her yourself."

Finn holds out his phone to me, and I blink. I'm almost afraid to take it. But when I hold it to my ear, Finn's green eyes are steady on me and the same sense of calm descends as when he has me tied up, in his power.

"Hi?"

"I'm Duncan Blackstone, Miss Harewood?" says male voice in a broad Scottish accent.

"For now," Finn rumbles.

"That's right." Am I answering the man on the phone or the one in front of me?

"I understand you've been kidnapped," says Duncan.

I flick my gaze to Finn's.

He spreads his hands. "You did it first."

"It's complicated," I reply.

"I had a fuck-buddy marriage to my daughter's best friend who I was secretly in love with, and she secretly felt the same. Try me," he says, Scottish accent bone dry.

Finn snorts with laughter.

"Okay, you know about complicated," I acknowledge. "What happened was..." I think about telling Duncan that I accidentally kidnapped Finn, and then Finn captured me back, then we've spent six days together and I think I've fallen in love with him. "Basically, the same thing."

My captor grins.

"You've got married?" the Scot asks sceptically.

"No," I correct him. "Not exactly." It's just that I know about secret love now.

"I can propose, anytime you want, pet." Finn winks and my heart gallops. He doesn't mean it. We're going back to London tomorrow, and this is his compensation for me kidnapping the playboy kingpin. A fun and sexy escapade.

"Look, I'll cut to the chase. The London Mafia Syndicate aims to reduce kidnappings. For some reason," he adds under his breath. "And we assume since he's missing, and so are you, that he's kidnapped you."

Neither Finn nor I say anything. I'm certainly not telling this Blackstone character that Finn allowed me to kidnap *him* for funsies.

"Is Kilburn holding you against your will?"

I hold Finn's gaze, and words clog in my throat.

A seagull squawks as it wheels around in the fading light as the sun sets.

"Miss?" Duncan asks when I don't reply for long seconds. "Where are you?"

"At a cottage by the sea that won't be mine in two days." The despair catches me by the gut again, dragging me down even as Finn slowly shakes his head, and I can't understand why.

"Look." The Scot sighs impatiently. "Is this a kinky sex thing, or do you want to get away?"

"You can run, but I'll catch you, pet."

Duncan's accent leaves me cold, but Finn's Irish accent? The thrill that shoots through me rocks me back on my heels. It's unreal. A smile plays around Finn's mouth. He's so, so big. Next to the sea, no one should feel like a mountain. But Finn does.

"Those two things aren't necessarily different," I point out to Duncan.

"Like that, is it?" he replies with amusement. "In that case—"

The phone is plucked from my hand.

"Enough. We've got kinky chasing to do," Finn states, then hangs up and shoves the phone in his pocket. He grabs my chin. "You kidnapped me, I kidnapped you. That's even."

I gaze up at him in disbelief.

"Now pet, this is the new compensation deal. You want your cottage?" He shifts his hand across my cheek, and down my neck before encircling my throat.

"Yes," I breathe. With his fingers around my neck, I really do feel like his leashed pet.

"Reach the house before I catch you and it's yours, no strings attached."

"What, really?" Wasn't that what I most wanted a lifetime ago when I was driving up here with a man I thought was Noah in the back of my car?

"I'll give you ten seconds before I chase. Get into the cottage and you can drive back to London. I should probably say that you can have some boring little life without me, I'll look after your brother, and let you go."

I'm shaking my head, but there's no need, because Finn gives me a roguish grin.

"But I won't. All that will happen is we'll play a longer game until you admit that you're mine."

My heart is fluttering like a caged bird.

His.

He lowers his voice to a rough growl and presses his fingers into the back of my neck, hard and possessive. "Whereas if I catch you, I'm going to hold you down, fuck you, and put a baby into you."

15

FINN

Her mouth falls open.

"I'm going to make you mine in every way. I will hold you down and take everything you've promised with those pretty eyes of yours since you first looked across the pub at me."

The savage beast in my chest roars with approval at this plan.

It's sunset. The sky is stained red and casting us into shadow. Millie's blonde hair is tinged pink. She's looking at me warily, as though uncertain I mean what I said.

"Go on then. *Run.*"

She blinks and for a second I think she might argue. Then she's dashing away over the sand. Her feet kick behind her and my cock thickens and heats as I watch her. My pet.

I give her a head start while I rip off my T-shirt then follow.

"When I catch you, I'm going to hold you down and make you pay," I call after her and she shrieks, glancing over her shoulder, her ponytail streaming behind her. She's unutterably beautiful.

Her legs pump faster, and I have to accelerate to keep up. And my god, chasing her down is as good as stalking her. Better, even, because she's in sight, close enough to touch very soon. And hunting down my pet is my new favourite game.

She's going to be *mine*.

16

MILLIE

I sprint along the beach, my mind racing as fast as my legs, some base instinct and fear triggered by Finn growling at me and telling me to run.

And the husky promise of what he'll do if he catches me —when he catches me—surges through my arteries as strongly as the blood and adrenaline.

Why am I running? Do I really just want my parents' cottage back, and a sane, normality? The lonely life.

My feet slip on the sand. Waves sweep up the shore.

I keep running.

The cottage that is all remaining of parents who never loved Noah and me enough to put us first, and ultimately left us without the care we needed.

I thought I was upset about losing the cottage, but am I? Really? Or was it only the symbol of what I believed could have been, if only everything had been different.

My arms flail as the beach opens up around me, the endless empty space of the calm sea to one side, and the shadows of the forest on the other. I'm so exposed here, but Finn is just behind.

"I'm coming for you, pet," he calls, his deep voice reverberating eerily through the half-darkness.

Panic grips me, making my legs move quicker. The simple movement allows my mind to clear in a way it hasn't for months. I've been tied up in a mess of knots, not knowing where to turn to since my brother started gambling more seriously.

My feet pound the sand, and my head is gloriously empty of doubt.

Finn would give me the cottage, I'm certain of that, if I can just get inside.

Finn Kilburn calmly allowed me to kidnap him, and rescued Noah. He gave me what I didn't even know I wanted, ignited desires I've never needed until now.

"That's it, run," Finn calls, and he's closer than I expected, sparking me to push more.

My legs are burning, my chest heaving. I can't get in air quickly enough, dragging it in desperately as I keep moving myself forward, towards the cottage.

"A baby."

Oh my god. That.

He does want to have sex with me. Was he holding back all this time we've spent together? I can't think why, but there's no mistaking him now.

"The first of many. We Irish do love to have big families." Heat thuds between my legs as I run.

My heart is so light I feel like it's lifting me upwards. Like I might float away from being so happy. It's Finn. This man is everything I never dared confess to myself or anyone else that I wanted. After a lifetime of taking care of my brother, and making up for our parents being careless, someone wants to look after me.

I don't even have to make decisions, or be good. He's

happy to take charge, and after caring for Noah my whole life and patients at work, I love that he does.

"I'm going to get you," he rasps and he's right behind me. The shock makes me stumble on the sand, but somehow, I catch myself and continue sprinting. How he didn't snatch hold as I slowed, I don't know.

But I don't look back. I train my eyes on the cottage.

The door is there, open for me to enter through, and take my prize.

"Millie." He's a breath away.

I'm feet from the cottage door.

I can do it. I can get through.

I could make this place mine again, a solace and a reminder of what I didn't lose because I never really had it.

Family. Love.

Or I could veer to the side, and run alongside the stone walls of the house and towards the forest, and belong to the man who held me and listened and stroked my hair as I told him every heavy secret in my heart. And who made me sob with pleasure.

It's no more than a thought, then a pair of strong arms catch me around my waist, snatching me up to a hard chest that's above my shoulder blades. A big, muscled Irishman.

Finn.

He's caught me.

I'm his.

17

FINN

We're both breathing hard as I trap her with my arms against the wall of the cottage.

"You slowed. You didn't catch me on the sand when you could have," she says in awe.

I cup her jaw and press my forehead to hers. "You could have gone through the door into the house. You turned."

She doesn't deny it. She can't, anymore than I can. This thing between us is too strong. It's the tide, pushing us up the beach inch by inch. While we aren't watching, the force of nature that is our connection keeps lapping closer.

"Why did you let me go on the beach?" she says instead of admitting she wanted to be caught.

Because it has to be her decision to be with me. It might be inevitable as far as I'm concerned, but when I fuck her, I want to know that she's with me.

But that's not the only reason, and it's not what she needs to hear right now.

"Because I like the chase. I liked seeing you scared, and running, and thinking you couldn't escape me." Her chest is heaving, and her eyes go wide, but as she trembles and leans back against the stone wall, it's not fear in her eyes. It's relief. My girl needs to be overpowered. I can do that for her. Be the dominant protector she needs. "And you needed to think you had a chance. That and I didn't want to fuck you for the first time on the beach. Sand isn't the right kind of friction."

"No?" she asks, voice breathy.

"The friction I want is my cock deep in your tight little virgin pussy," I murmur, rolling my hips against her. And she pushes back into me, her soft belly yielding to the rigid length of my cock. I lean down and our mouths touch.

The passion I've held back is unleashed. My lips force hers open in a possessive kiss. My tongue is in her mouth, and she's moaning as I shift my hands to hold her delicious curves as I devour her.

I kiss her like she's my source of air. And she is.

I crowd her between my body and the stone, loving the way that even as I trap her, she tries to get closer, reaching up and tugging on my shoulders. Our movements have rucked up that perfect little sundress, and I'm tempted, oh so tempted to take her out here against the wall.

And I will.

One day, I'll give in to every feral impulse and thrust into my wife while holding her against the sun-warmed stone. But today? She's not yet my wife, and her first time will be for *her*. As sweet as my virgin girl needs, and no more pain than absolutely necessary.

"There's one thing you need to know, Millie," I say, pulling back to stare into her face, so familiar now and so beloved.

She nods, panting, her lips bruised pink and shiny with our saliva in the light of the setting sun.

"Two, actually." My throat closes up. I shouldn't say

this. I should just take what she's offering and never reveal my true self. But my pet deserves more. She should have honesty.

"I want you. I want you more than my next breath. I want you with the ferocity of a man in the desert craving water and shade. I will die without you."

She brings up her hand and places it on my cheek, her pretty blue eyes shining into mine, and murmurs, "It's okay, I feel the same."

That should comfort me. But it doesn't.

"And that's why..."

Tilting her head, she waits.

"I stalked you."

18

MILLIE

"Stalked?" I echo in disbelief.

"More like self-appointed as your invisible personal cheerleader and protection detail."

He was there, watching over me, and now he's making a joke? God, I love this man.

"You bastard," I say, in awe.

"Sorry." But he doesn't look sorry, and he doesn't let me go.

"I thought I was going *mad*." All those times I thought I was seeing him? The moments my skin prickled as though I was being observed, but when I turned no one was there?

"I know, I'm sorry."

It's only when he leans his cheek into my hand that I realise I've dug my nails into his skin, and he's accepting it, like I'm a kitten using her claws unknowingly.

"I needed to see you, and know more about you," he continues, then presses his lips to my palm, kissing me softly, in a balance to the harshness of my hold on him.

"You're not as invisible as you think." I sound annoyed.

I guess I am. I knew there was something weird going on. "At what, six foot—"

"Five, yeah. I stand out. I couldn't stay away, Millie."

"Not subtle." I try to smile. "Do you always get caught?"

"Stalking?"

"Yeah, by the other women you follow." The words are like chewing glass.

"Never," he replies quickly. "You're the only one who has ever seen me."

Well, that's something, I tell myself as my heart crumples a bit. This is fine. Right?

"Because I don't do it," he continues. "I've never stalked anyone before."

"Oh," I breathe. My heart puffs back up to full size, then expands further at the inference I'm special. "I thought maybe lots of women—"

"You're not one of many, pet," he cuts me off, and hauls me closer to him, like he's attempting to melt our clothes off with the pressure. "Or the latest. You're the last, and the first. The only woman I'll have in bed for the rest of my life, and the first I've needed to be with like this."

Happiness radiates out of my chest.

"No wonder you weren't very good," I joke.

"I did most of it by having CCTV hacked." He shrugs.

"Most of it wasn't in person?" I splutter. "And I still saw you!"

He has the grace to look sheepish. "I can't hide from you."

"The playboy kingpin stalked a girl rather than just picking from one of his admirers?" I murmur.

"I told you the truth days ago. I haven't even kissed anyone for years, Millie. It's all an act."

I ease my fingertips and slide my hand to the back of his bowed head, and his short hair is like velvet.

Part of me is still scared. I don't trust that I'm lovable. After all, my family has never really cared about me.

But I trust him.

And suddenly it's so clear, and all my fears seem ridiculous. He followed me, he allowed me to kidnap him, he's cooked me three hot meals a day since we've been here. He watched me, yes.

He *sees* me.

He caught me, and says that he loves me. But far more than that, he has *shown* me that he cares.

"I'll always see you," I murmur.

"Millie," he groans, then leans down and kisses me. He wraps his arms around me and carries me into the cottage, kicking the door closed behind us. His mouth doesn't leave mine as he charges up the steep stairs like they're nothing.

He tosses me onto the bed, and I bounce on the mattress with an "Oof!" and the ruthless energy of it is intoxicating.

"Take your clothes off. Now," he demands, ripping his T-shirt over his head.

I'm momentarily stunned—maybe I always will be—by the beauty of his naked chest. Then he's shoving down his jeans, revealing his cock, and even though he's huge, I want him. He's throbbing, erect, and gorgeous enough to make me beg.

"Pet." His warning snaps me out of my inaction, and I wriggle out of my sundress as he gazes at me, lazily stroking his cock as I peel off my knickers and bra. He steps closer, looking down at me and I'm deliciously exposed.

I see the moment he notices the cuffs on the bedside cabinet, still where he left them. His gaze flicks back to my wrists.

"Forgive me, my love," he says and reaches for them. "But you doubt that I want you, worrying about my past? I'm going to show you that I'm not letting go of you."

He snatches my wrist before I can even reply, and deliberately lifts it over my head.

"Ever." He loops the cuff around the slats of the headboard.

My breath catches. This is new.

"Pink fluffy handcuffs," Finn muses as he clicks the second handcuff shut. "Did you think when you bought them about me putting them on you?"

Yes. And I tried not to, because I was ashamed. "No?"

Finn narrows his eyes. "Do you like to say no when you mean yes, pet?"

Why do I feel guilty about this? The voices in my head that say I should be good and restrained and not be so selfish as to have pleasure for its own sake, or anything just for me, are still there. And the idea of getting pregnant, after only knowing this man for a matter of days?

I can almost hear my mother clicking her tongue and muttering.

"No?"

He laughs softly. "Choose a safe word."

"What?"

"A word that I know means stop, and I'll stop and take care of you. But otherwise, I won't. I'll do exactly what I want to you, use your cute little body in filthy and degrading ways, fuck every hole until you can't move without memory of me echoing through you."

Heat floods me. Between my legs tingles with pure need, and I have vague pictures in my mind of Finn gleefully fucking me as I scream my heart out, free to beg and sob and shout that I don't want this overwhelming pleasure that forces me to do nothing but accept the orgasms.

I... I can't want that, can I?

"And you know what else, pet?"

I shake my head, because I don't know. I will listen to anything Finn tells me though.

His voice dips and he brings his mouth to my ear. "I won't use protection like a kind and tame psychopath would."

My pussy clenches.

"Nothing but your safe word will stop me. I'd take you raw. I'd push my far-too-big cock into your tight virgin passage and fill you up. I'd make my come spill out of your gorgeous little cunt, then force in more. I'd push it back in, and make you hold it. I'd force you to go outside with my seed dribbling down your legs like the little slut you are."

I'm panting, sensation flaring over my skin and down my spine.

"I'll fuck a baby into you. I'll be insatiable, Millie. I'll part your thighs whenever I want and shove into you, grab your breasts and hold you down as I defile you in ways you haven't even begun to imagine. And you will take it all."

My hips move of their own accord, my clit throbbing. My nipples are aching.

I'm shaking with the need for what Finn describes. And when he calls me a slut? It sounds like a *compliment*. It sounds like he'll celebrate every selfish thing I do and all the ways I let him have control so I don't have to do anything.

The thought is a helium balloon inside my mind.

I need him.

But I can't say yes. Years and years of being a good girl who looked after everyone has taken its toll.

I like being Finn's prisoner. Madness, but true. I trust him and it's such a relief for him to be in charge.

"And the only thing between you and me and my insatiable lust is one little word, pet. And it's not no. I won't take no for an answer, because you saw me outside your brother's work and kidnapped me anyway."

"I didn't—"

"You did," he insists roughly. "You knew it was me. In here." He slams his palm between my breasts. "You knew it was me, and you wanted this, so you captured me. You needed this as much as I did."

Is that true?

I *did* have a flash of knowledge that it wasn't Noah there. And I didn't check.

I chose not to look into his face and ensure it was Noah I pushed into my car.

"So unless you tell me in a word that we've agreed means no more, I'm not going to stop until you're wrung out with pleasure and have a baby in your belly."

"No." It tears from my throat.

He growls.

I like saying that far too much. It's the perfect abdication of responsibility.

"Choose one. Now."

My mind goes blank. This is that BDSM thing, isn't it? I've always been the good girl, the responsible one. Never Googled all those spicy terms. Never allowed myself to wonder when people turned up at the hospital with red cheeks and unusual injuries in intimate places.

"Millie." He sounds furious, and that only makes me hotter.

"Ocean." I don't know where that word emerges from.

But it's right. The ocean is big—too big. It's what you drown in.

"Ocean," he repeats. "Good girl. Well done."

I glow from his praise.

"Are you ready to have me pound into your tight pussy?"

"No." And the shake of fear isn't pretend. He is enormous. I'll never be fully ready.

He abruptly cups between my legs. "This says otherwise, pet."

"No." It's not my fault. I'm not responsible for anything that happens, I can just accept everything that Finn gives me. I have wings. I'm flying. I have gills. I can breathe underwater.

"You're soaking wet," he rasps.

"Please." Am I begging for him to stop? Or carry on?

"I know, I know." He notches the thick head of his cock at my entrance. "Feck, you're so slippery. Feel how hard you make me, pet?"

He pushes into me, and I make a high-pitched cry as the intrusion pinches. "I can't, I can't," I babble. "It's too big."

"Breathe, pet," he instructs, harsh but tender at the same time, keeping pushing further into me, and another scream rips from my throat. "You will. Feel how big you make my cock? How much I need to fuck you. You were made for me."

It hurts, but my brain doesn't register the pain properly. It's a cascade of sparks that are so bright and hot that it feels almost pleasurable. After a second, it eases. I instantly want him deeper, and he's relentless. I know he's not going as fast as he'd like, and I'm both grateful for his consideration and impatient that his monster cock isn't fully in yet.

We both let out an "Ahhh" as he holds my hip down

and slides further, making me take it exactly as I wanted. This time the flare of pain isn't as sharp. And more quickly it's fullness, and an unfamiliar stretch, and I'm vibrating because I want him so much.

He doesn't stop. He continues to slide in endlessly until he hits my heart.

It's not my heart, but it feels high enough that it could be. Then his hips are flush with mine and his balls press onto my bottom and he seamlessly begins to withdraw.

"Feck you're so tight," he rasps. "My hot, wet little toy. My beautiful love, my pet."

He's so controlled as he moves in and out of me, just his hips moving without hesitation. And he's close to me in a way I can't imagine being with anyone else. Finn is inside me. Making space for his thick cock.

I moan as he speeds up, using my body for his pleasure, and I can see how good it is for him. The intensity in his green eyes only wavers from my face to appreciate my bared breasts.

I can't touch him, but I'm enough without doing anything.

It's perfect.

19

FINN

This is going to kill me.

Not a bullet or a knife, not the Essex Cartel or some upstart in Kilburn. Not too much whiskey or one last roast potato with too much butter. Nope. This perfect woman will be my downfall.

My blood feels like a cocktail of innocent drugs that add up to more than I thought possible. As addictive as heroin, but pure and sweet as sugar. Being in my girl's pussy is the sort of high that you think because it's natural and legal isn't dangerous.

But Millie is fatal. Nothing will ever be as good as being joined with her.

"I love you." That's the fecking least of it, but they're the words that most simply express the endless emotion in my heart.

"I love you too," she pants out, and I grin.

"Yes, fall apart for me." She's an addiction of the best kind, that makes me want to be a better man for her. I'll never tire of feeling her come, be it on my fingers, my tongue, or—best of all—my cock.

"I can't."

"I'll break you then," I croon as I let go of her thigh and cup her breast, dragging my thumb over her nipple. She jerks and I can't get enough of that. I repeat, then roll the sensitive little point between my fingers. "You will scream and strangle my cock twice before I pump you full."

She writhes beneath me, tugging at her hands.

"I might get pregnant." She's breathless.

"Oh, you will. I'm going to breed you. Make you swollen with my baby so I can show off what a good girl my fertile little wife is, taking all my seed."

"I'm not your wife," she replies, disbelievingly.

"You will be." I slam into her hard this time, once, then again. My balls tingle as they swing against her soft little arse. "Just as you're my love, and my whole life, already."

"I..." Angles her hips up for more, and moans.

"That's it, open for me more, pet." I stroke her knee as I slowly increase the speed of my thrusts. I watch her and my own arousal is second to the satisfaction of seeing how hot and squirmy she's getting. Her cheeks are flushed.

"You're so fecking tight. Spread your legs wider, my beautiful girl," I grunt, watching to see her response, and she doesn't disappoint. She mewls and as I thrust again, it's wetter. But she's so far gone, she can't think to move quickly for me. I grab her thigh, and push it out and upwards.

Her eyes go unfocused, and her eyelids flutter closed as the angle changes, and it's even better, I can tell.

"Finn, I..."

Then she's tightening around my cock. The pleasure is building to a point I can't control myself. She's my whole world, and I need to blow my load into her and put a baby in her belly.

My balls pull up and I grit my teeth. The only thing

that's keeping me from the animalistic pounding into her that will tip me over is wanting her to know everything about how obsessed I am with her. How much I love her and need her in my life. I want no doubts, even as we're playing that I'm forcing her.

Grabbing her jaw, I press my fingers into the side of her neck and tilt her head until she looks into my eyes.

"Let me be your shelter from every storm, and your shade on scorching days. I'll be your blanket when you're cold, and your seat when you're tired."

"I can't sit on you!" she chokes out.

"You can. You will. You'll sit on my face and pedal my ears like a good girl until you squirt, and I lick it up because it's nectar."

She giggles, but she's shaking too.

I let her jaw go and reach down for her clit as my own breathing goes ragged. Her squeak of surprise as I cram my hand between us makes me smile savagely. Such a lot to learn, my girl. She has no idea how this will be.

"I love you, I have from the very start. And I'm going to take such fecking good care of you, you'll be my happy little captive."

"Finn," she moans, writhing as I find her clit and stroke it.

"Barefoot." I kiss her. "And pregnant." Another soft kiss as I fuck her hard. "And loved. Cherished." I graze my teeth over her lower lip. "Spoiled to within an inch of your life." I suck her bottom lip, and she writhes beneath me as I keep it captured.

All the time I'm thrusting into her and rubbing insistent circles onto her clit.

"You're not getting away without another orgasm, Millie. You know that, yeah?"

"Mmm!" she whines.

"That's right, pet. Come for me. Your stalker is going to give you a baby."

She sobs, thrashing almost as though she wants to get me off her. But she doesn't kick me, and she doesn't say the word. So I kiss her and tangle the fingers of one hand in her hair as the other insists that she come with harder and harder movements over that sensitive little nub.

"You can't do anything to stop me. Beg, plead. I don't care. I have to have you."

I'm hanging on by a thread.

"When I watched you on the hospital CCTV, I dreamed of being this close to you. Of being inside you." It's even better than I fantasised as I jerked off to the image of Millie, night after lonely night. "You're so perfect, I want to live like this. Joined together."

And maybe that's what triggers her orgasm, because I have to grit my teeth as she grips me so tightly it's as though she's trying to break my cock right off. But feck, it feels amazing.

"Good girl." My chest heaves, and I still. Because despite everything, this has to last a little longer.

There's more I need from my pet.

20

MILLIE

I want him to lose control. I need him to be as crazy and unhinged as I know he can be. I want to be the one person who makes him crazy.

"Finn, release me."

His expression goes feral, and yeah, that's the vibe.

"Please," I whisper.

"Never." It's a hard word. "You're mine." He punctuates the statement with thrusts. "My good girl. Mine to breed. You can't stop your stalker—"

"Finn! I love you and I want to touch you!" I almost yell, tugging at my cuffs.

He stills, and no, no, this restraint isn't what I want.

"You're not getting away," he murmurs, still sliding his thick cock in and out of me, teeth gritted.

"I don't want to. I'll never leave. I'm yours. I always was."

A conflicted look crosses his face. "One more orgasm—"

"No! I need you to come inside me right now. I've…" I can't describe how I'm fulfilled by being what he needs, but I've had my care. Now I need the full force of his love, and to show him mine. No game of being forced to accept pleasure. I enjoyed it, it was satisfying, I needed it even.

But now I need something even more raw. Honesty.

He reaches up, and without pulling his cock out of me, grabs the key from the bedside cabinet and releases my hands.

I touch him. Gentle, loving fingers over his shoulder and neck, over the necklaces he told me were gifts from his family, up to where the dark sandpaper of his short beard begins. Then my other hand is free, and I'm touching him everywhere I can reach. Greedy to show with my eagerness how much he means to me.

"Finn, my Finn."

"I'm yours," he agrees, then wraps his arms around me and before I know it, he's rolled us over so I'm on top.

Cautiously, I lever myself up, and shift on his cock. We both moan, and this angle is different, but Finn likes it, I can tell. I experimentally move up and down. He's making noises like it's painful, and his forehead is creased between his eyebrows.

"Millie, I love you so fecking much," he says, under his breath. He cups my breasts roughly and yes, oh yes. That's an advantage of me on top and untethered that I hadn't anticipated.

He doesn't make me do all the work though. He thrusts up into me as I bear down, his stomach muscles flexing under that happy trail of hair.

"I love you." It's so simple, and yet it took something pretty significant to get us to this point.

"Beautiful," he mutters indistinctly, and trails his hands down my torso, his palms covering my whole belly. He grips my hips, and lifts me in time with his movements, and it's deeper, harder, sweeter. I cry out as I can feel him deep inside. He fills a space I didn't know existed.

But he still hasn't really lost his mind. I want him to come inside me without a thought for *me*.

It's an instinct, but I reach behind and feel for his big balls.

He swears as my fingers touch his sack.

"I won't last if you do that, pet," he grits out.

"Good." I'm in a haze of pleasure and need.

I cup his balls, feeling their weight.

"Pull on them."

He's the most savagely beautiful thing I've ever seen as he throws his head back and shudders, keeping my gaze all the while. Then I do as he directs, and he swells, slamming my hips down on his. And while him on top of me was amazing, him using me from below, like he's the endless sea and I'm a little boat, is even better.

He roars his release. The shout is so loud and long I think they'll hear it in Kilburn.

He pumps into me, and I feel that hot seed hitting my insides, filling me up, his cock jerking over and over.

Then he's pulling me down to slump over his chest, and murmuring that I'm his good girl, perfect girl, his pet, and stroking my hair.

We lie there for a long time, still joined, my face pressed onto his pectoral and his arms tight around my shoulders.

Maybe I fall asleep, exhausted by sheer happiness? Because the next thing I know, there's the soft clink of metal on metal. I struggle to comprehend what it means.

"Millie," he whispers, sweeping my hair away and brushing his lips on my forehead. "It's more usual to do this on one knee, but I can't wait. And nothing about this has been traditional."

That wakes me up.

"What?"

I wriggle against his chest until I get my arms under me enough to be able to stare into his eyes. They're still impossibly green. They're a jungle, but I can see love and amusement in them all the same.

And then I see what he's holding. The ring that was on one of the chains around his neck. He told me it was his grandfather's. One of the tokens of his family he wears at all times.

"Do you want to marry me?" I blurt out, my disbelief stronger than my good sense.

That wicked twinkle is back in his eyes. "Yes. I accept."

My mouth falls open. "I wasn't asking!" I protest. "I was asking if you were ask—"

"Weren't you?" His hand finds mine and slides the ring —still warm from his skin—over my finger. It's too big, but my fingers close over it. I want to keep this. I want to be kept by him. "Well, it's a good thing I *am* asking."

"Finn." I haven't got words for this. He brings our linked hands up between us and to his lips, then kisses my palm. It sends a shudder of pleasure down my spine.

"You don't have any option, Millie," he says with quiet intent. "You're mine. I'm yours. I'm going to keep you forever and put a baby in you. I probably already have."

Dragging my hand down his face, when my forefinger slides over his lips, he opens his mouth and catches it, closing over the tip. Then the wet heat of his mouth surrounds the tip, and his teeth close like a trap, digging into my flesh. I moan as a fresh wave of arousal crashes over me.

"I could consume you," he murmurs. "I want all of you. A wedding is just the formal tags. My ring on your finger— this one for now, but I'll get you a custom-made engagement ring. Something designed for my beautiful pet, to remind you of the sea, and where you brought me to let me take everything you give and more."

He pulls me flush against him with his lower arm, but keeps our hands interlocked as he kisses me, his lips just as perfect as I imagined when we first met.

"Kidnapping you was the best choice I ever made," I whisper.

His chest vibrates as he laughs. "Most fun I've ever had."

21

MILLIE

A FEW DAYS LATER

"Sis." Noah looks at me like I'm a ghost as Finn and I walk into the wing of Finn's enormous house that Noah has been staying in while I fell in love with his boss. "What are you doing here?"

We've only just arrived back, and the therapist messaged that Noah needed to see me, so of course we came straight to see him. I'm not worried. I'm not.

Except what if his treatment isn't going as well as we thought.

"She's marrying me," Finn says, dropping a kiss on the top of my head. His arm is around my waist. He hasn't stopped touching me, even now he knows I love him and I'm not going to leave him.

He likes it, I've realised. All of this was only ever because he loved me.

Noah, though, is white.

"Millie." His voice trembles. "What did you have to do—?"

I can't help but giggle at his evident fear. Finn? Scary? I can't imagine it anymore. "Nothing, nothing," I assure him. "It's all good."

His gaze flits between Finn and me. "What happened?"

"Your sister kidnapped me, I convinced her to marry me," Finn replies matter-of-factly. "And in about nine months, you'll be an uncle."

I nod, because yeah. Undeniably true.

Noah visibly shakes himself. "What about your job?"

"Oh, we discussed that." Last night in bed, actually, after we were both exhausted. "I'm going to run the clinic for all the Kilburn men and their families."

"With plenty of help, so you don't end up caring for everyone at the expense of yourself," Finn reminds me in a low growl, and squeezes my waist.

Noah rubs his jaw, in disbelief.

"And we're going to have lots of kids," I add cheerfully.

"I can't believe..." Noah chokes a laugh and turns to Finn. "Is this why you insisted I sort myself out?"

"Sure look, you're a good barman." Finn shrugs. "For a gobshite. And our kids will need an uncle."

I snort, because with Finn's six brothers and sisters, our children will hardly be lacking uncles. Finn did this for me.

"That's a great reason to get myself solvent," Noah grins. "Because in a few years I need to be able to give my niece or nephew a drum kit."

I groan but can't help laughing. "They are not going to have drum kits!"

"They will if Uncle Noah gives them to them," my brother says gleefully.

"Mm." Finn makes a dark rumble from the back of his throat. "In which case, we'll need a padded cell."

"I think he means an isolation booth," I reassure an immediately wary Noah. "One of those rooms with foam on the walls so you and your nieces and nephews don't disturb anyone with your music."

"That's grand." Finn nods. "Exactly what I meant. We'll leave you to your work."

He tugs my waist and heat pulses through me. He promised me ten minutes to check up on my brother before he wanted to take me to *his* bed, that is apparently the right size for giants like him. Turns out, he's had cold feet every night we spent at the cottage because the bed is too small.

"Sis... I, there's something..." Noah starts as we turn away, then hesitates. "I'm sorry."

"You don't—" I begin.

"You should be," Finn says over me.

"About everything," Noah adds at the same time. "That's why I needed to see you. To say... Sorry."

The last bit of tension I was holding slips away. His therapist is dealing with Noah's addiction now. I don't have to. And my brother is sorry.

I smile. If he hadn't been in such a bad place, would I have met Finn? "It's okay."

It's more than okay, as Finn guides me through his modern home, bright paintings on the walls and thick carpets underfoot. This turned out better than I could have dreamed.

But Finn sees something in my eyes as he pauses by a door. He takes my chin between his thumb and forefingers and examines my face. "You wanted to save him and fix the problem."

"Saviour complex," I agree. "But he's in safe hands now."

"Mmm." He leans down and kisses me, pulling me into his bedroom before kicking the door shut behind us. "What you really wanted was for someone to care for *you*."

I melt into him, not even looking at the room. All I can see is Finn.

"And it's me," he continues. "I'm proud to be the support you need, Millie. You're strong, but I'm stronger, pet."

"Harder, that's for sure." I push back against the thickening length pressing into my belly.

His chest vibrates as he laughs, and it's the best feeling in the world.

EPILOGUE
FINN

7 Years later

I'm back at the table in the pub where everything started. The big round table at the back, with a clear view of the bar. And there's great craic, no question.

"Daddy, it's your go!" our eldest daughter, Aisling tells me.

I'm sitting with the kids playing a fierce game of Monopoly, and watching my wife like the stalker I am at heart.

"Sorry, Aisling." I refocus on the board. I'm the top hat, and I'm in jail. As per usual.

"You're distracted," our middle daughter, Fia, points out.

"I'm paying attention now." But it's a lie. My gaze slides up to where Millie is on the phone at bar.

Our toddler Lana is sitting on the other side of the table, colouring in something pink. She loves pink. And our baby boy, Cillian, is asleep in a wrap thing that straps him to my chest.

Sunday mornings used to be a no-go for me. When I was young, because I'd be in bits from drinking too much on Saturday night, and probably avoiding whoever I'd slept with. Then when I stopped those shite habits, I hated them for the emptiness of having no one around to distract me from the hollowness inside me.

They're my favourite now, because there's no business to be attended to, no school, no London Mafia Syndicate, and I can spend time with my family. No distractions.

Except when my wife has been called by her friend from the London Mafia Smut Club for an emergency chat about the new book that released two days ago, and her friend *has to* talk spoilers with someone. Right now, because she stayed up all night reading.

Millie said no, but I told her we could play our old game while she chatted, and I played with the kids.

"Daddyyy!" Aisling's complaint is echoed by Fia this time.

I grin. "Alright. Better pay and get out of jail. Even a bad man can't stay locked up forever."

I hand over the notes to Fia, who is acting as the bank, and Aisling narrows her eyes. "I thought you said you didn't have enough money to buy your way out?"

"Are you accusing me of lying?" I reply.

She pouts. "Yes."

I wink at her, then slide my gaze over to Millie. "Sometimes, imprisoned is the best place to be."

EXTENDED EPILOGUE
FINN

"Knees," I growl as I shut the bedroom door behind me.

But my good girl is already there, waiting for me.

"Sir," she murmurs and despite having been with our kids only seconds ago, my cock is surging to the occasion. Thickening to a hard length that I'm going to force down my wife's throat until she screams. But I know Millie now. In a way that I couldn't be sure of her when we were first in the little cottage together, and I almost used her pretty mouth without thought, but stopped myself.

There's no need to stop.

In a few long paces I'm in front of her, and grab her hair, pulling her head back, she gives a whimper as my fingers tighten.

"I'm going to fuck your mouth until I come down your throat." I free my cock with my other hand, then slap my cock against her plush bottom lip. "Open up."

She opens immediately, with a gasp of anticipation.

I slide into the silken hot wetness of her mouth, in and in until I hit the back, and the pleasure is so intensely right, my knees go weak.

There's no hesitation. She's mine to use. I never doubt it.

"I missed you," I whisper, drawing back and thrusting in harder. Even though it's only been a day with my family, and without the utter privacy we take for granted in our house at Kilburn, I still miss being able to close a door and have my wife entirely to myself, with no risk of being overheard.

She grips my thighs through my hastily shoved down trousers, and tilts her head to open her throat. The next thrust in, she takes me to the hilt, my balls slapping under her chin, and it feels like she's setting my every pleasure-sensing neuron on fire. I cup the back of her neck, clenching my fists in her hair to hold her still, and go harder.

"Suck me," I demand, voice hoarse. "Feel how hard you make me. How much you turn me on, even after all these years together."

She makes a whining noise from her nose and digs her nails into the muscles of my thighs. And then she does as I say, her lips sealing as best they can around my cock.

The bliss spikes, pooling at the base of my spine.

"Good girl. You're being such a good girl for me."

We've been training for years to be able to do this, and she's amazing. Millie knows that sometimes I just need to use her. And if the way it gets her soaked between the legs is anything to judge by, she needs it too. She loves it.

I fuck her mouth ruthlessly. She's my toy, my love, the object of all my desires. Millie is the woman I worship and the person I need most in the world.

My wife.

I fuck her like I hate her, unmoved even as tears leak from her eyes and drip onto that expensive, slinky dress.

The urge to come all over her, to mark her, is there, a

mere scratch beneath the surface. Possessiveness is part of me, all the way to the bone. She's mine, and everyone in the country knows it. Kilburn, London, Britain, Ireland.

All our children aren't enough. Millie is still the most stunning creature I've ever seen, and I know how lucky I am. A woman fifteen years younger than me loves me and kneels eagerly for me, taking my cock any way I want her to.

"You're such a good girl," I tell her as I slam into her hot, wet mouth. "You like it, don't you? The feel of me using you."

She tries to nod, but fails, holding my thighs in a death grip—the only signal she has right now to reply.

She's a slut for me, and naughty too.

"Good fecking girl. Best fecking girl."

I'm losing it.

I'm going to shoot my load.

And my wife knows me far too well. One hand—not both or she knows I'd stop—releases from my thigh and creeps up to where I'm hammering into her mouth with barely a pause for her to breathe. She encircles the base of my cock, her fingers failing to meet, and adds her hand to the already overwhelming sensation.

I choke. My balls pull up.

The little minx must feel that too.

"Millie," I groan.

The push of my underwear away from my balls should be expected. Millie has teased me thousands of times that I have massive bollocks, and that she loves to see how much come she can milk from me. Yet, it always shocks me as taboo when she reaches to cup my balls in her little, smooth hand. Because she really wants it. My wife wants my come down her throat or in her cunt, or over her tits. She craves all of it.

I work my cock right at the tight back of her mouth, and I can barely breathe any better than she can. I can't tell her I'm going to come, or stop it when her fingers fit onto my sack, and tug down.

"Millie." I see stars. The orgasm is white-hot and takes over my whole body, but I manage to push out one word as I come. The one name that is my guiding light and my entire life.

Millie, my wife.

My eyes go hazy, and when she swallows down every burst of come, throat bobbing, it's like that triggers more. Four, five spurts. Then another. She drains me, and when she brings her hands to cover mine, my brain can't process anything but love and pleasure.

"That was amazing," I rasp. "Feck, Millie, that was—"

Then there's a click of metal, cool on my wrists.

She lifts my hands from her head, and I stare in shock.

My wife has handcuffed me.

Millie gives a satisfied sigh as she withdraws her mouth from my still-hard cock, a line of our combined spit and come drawing out then falling onto her chin.

"What the feck..." Then my orgasm-stupefied brain gets it.

"Time for a bit of payback," she replies, and I flick my gaze between my wife's face and my incapacitated hands as she stands.

Whenever I think we've reached our limits, Millie can always surprise me, or sometimes I can shock her.

I laugh with delight as I test the cuffs.

"They're new," she says with a smirk, catching me by the arm and guiding me towards the bed. "You won't wriggle out of them like the old pink fluffy ones.

"Leather." It's thick beneath my fingertips. "You think I

can't get out and punish you for being such a brat as to tie me up?"

"I know so." Her sassy look warms and relaxes me even more than coming in her mouth did.

"You had them made especially."

"Just for you, husband." She pushes me back, and I accept, falling onto the covers.

"Come here then," I groan. "Sit on my face and pedal my ears. Suffocate me, pet. Make me pleasure you over and over."

I'm never sure whether excessive numbers of orgasms are my punishment for her, or her treat from me.

She throws one leg over my torso and shimmies up. I urge her with my trapped hands against her little arse. I shove her forwards when she would sit politely on my chest.

"On my face," I grit out as she makes a sound of discontent.

Then her soft pink folds land on my tongue. Sweet and salt and the best thing I'll ever taste. And god, but she feels amazing too as I lap at her. The pressure of her on my chin is an ache that I love, taking a bit of pain for her.

She mews and shifts as I get to her clit and set up a solid rhythm.

I fecking love this side of Millie. It's as much of a turn-on when she's on top and grinding down to use my mouth or my cock as when I'm taking advantage of her pretty cunt, or we're equals just starving for each other.

I can't talk to urge her on, though I want to something fierce. My lips are pressed down by her pussy.

Beautiful. I adore caring for her.

If I drown, I'd die happy. If I suffocate, even better. I can't care when Millie is taking her pleasure, rolling her hips and riding my face, getting my determined tongue exactly where she needs it.

The cuffs are a frustration—I'd love to grab a handful of her tits and pinch her nipples to get her to a more intense release. But there's a kinky symmetry when she incapacitates me, and it turns me on that she wants me as much as I want her.

So even as my tongue screams at me to stop and her juices trickle down my cheeks, I'm fecking happy. I'm the happiest man alive to service my perfect wife. I worship her, laving her clit over and over, then sucking. And the more it hurts, the better I like it because Millie is coming apart, panting, writhing, her hands in my hair, tugging. I grew it out into longer curls just so she could do this whenever she likes.

"Finn!"

She crashes into orgasm and savage satisfaction sweeps through my body as I feel her pulse on my tongue.

Normally, I'd catch her as the aftershocks hit her, stroking her sides and her belly—the stretch marks we put there from her carrying our children are my current new favourite part of Millie—and gently working her through it.

But my hands are tied, so it's all up to her.

"Finn," she breathes again as she lifts herself from my aching jaw. She looks down into my face, and the sight of her dishevelled from coming, and her makeup has run from me fucking her mouth, makes me throb.

"Get onto my cock," I growl, my voice hardly my own and my tongue slow.

Her eyes go wide, but she obeys, shifting down, leaving a wet trail on my chest and arms until we line up. She takes my length in her hand, but it's me that thrusts upwards, right into her pussy.

And we both groan.

I'm pistoning up into her immediately, even as she moves more slowly, still sensitive after coming.

"I love you," I grit out. "I'm not going to last long."

"Fill me up." She falls forwards and, arms resting on my chest and my arms trapped between us as I pound up into her impossibly wet pussy, she frames my face with her hands and kisses me. "I love you. I love you so much."

"Millie." And that's the last word I manage before I fall again into ecstasy.

THANKS

Thank you for reading, I hope you enjoyed it.

Want to read a little more Happily Ever After? Click to get exclusive epilogues and free stories! or head to Evie-RoseAuthor.com

If you have a moment, I'd really appreciate a review wherever you like to talk about books. Reviews, however brief, help readers find stories they'll love.

Love to get the news first? Follow me on your favored social media platform - I love to chat to readers and you get all the latest gossip.

If the newsletter is too much like commitment, I recommend following me on BookBub, where you'll just get new release notifications and deals.

- amazon.com/author/evierose
- bookbub.com/authors/evie-rose
- instagram.com/evieroseauthor
- tiktok.com/@EvieRoseAuthor

INSTALOVE BY EVIE ROSE

Grumpy Bosses

Older Hotter Grumpier

My billionaire boss catches me reading when I should be working. And the punishment...?

Tall, Dark, and Grumpy

When my boss comes to fetch me from a bar, I'm expecting him to go nuts that I'm drunk and described my fake boyfriend just like him. But he demands marriage...

Silver Fox Grump

He was my teacher, and my first off-limits crush. Now he's my stalker, and my boss.

Stalker Kingpins

Spoiled by my Stalker

From the moment we lock eyes, I'm his lucky girl... But there's a price to pay

Kingpin's Baby

I beg the Kingpin for help... And he offers marriage.

Owned by her Enemy

I didn't expect the ruthless new kingpin—an older man, gorgeous and hard—to extract such a price for a ceasefire: an arranged marriage.

His Public Claim

My first time is sold to my brother's best friend

Accidentally Kidnapping the Mafia Boss

I might have kidnapped him, but the mafia boss isn't going to let me go.

Marrying the Boss

Baby Proposal

My boss walked in on me buying "magic juice" online... And now he's demanding to be my baby's daddy!

Groom Gamble

I accidentally gave my hot boss my list of requirements for a perfect husband: tall, gray eyes, nice smile, big d*ck. High sperm count.

London Mafia Bosses

Captured by the Mafia Boss

I might be an innocent runaway, but I'm at my friend's funeral to avenge her murder by the mafia boss: King.

Taken by the Kingpin

Tall, dark, older and dangerous, I shouldn't want him.

Stolen by the Mafia King

I didn't know he has been watching me all this time.

I had a plan to escape. Everything is going perfectly at my wedding rehearsal dinner until *he* turns up.

Caught by the Kingpin

The kingpin growls a warning that I shouldn't try his patience by attempting to escape.

There's no way I'm staying as his little prisoner.

Claimed by the Mobster

I'm in love with my ex-boyfriend's dad: a dangerous and powerful mafia boss twice my age.

Snatched by the Bratva

I have an excruciating crush on this man who comes into the coffee shop. Every day. He's older, gorgeous, perfectly dressed. He has a Russian accent and silver eyes.

Kidnapped by the Mafia Boss

I locked myself in the bathroom when my date pulled out a knife. Then a tall dark rescuer crashed through the door... and kidnapped me.

Held by the Bratva

"Who hurt you?"

Before I know it, my gorgeous neighbour has scooped me up into his arms and taken me to his penthouse. And he won't let me go.

Seized by the Mafia King

I'm kidnapped from my wedding

Abducted by the Mafia Don

"Touch her and die."

Filthy Scottish Kingpins

Forbidden Appeal

He's older and rich, and my teenage crush re-surfaces as I beg the former kingpin to help me escape a mafia arranged marriage. He stares at me like I'm a temptress he wants to banish, but we're snowed in at his Scottish castle.

Captive Desires

I was sent to kill him, but he's captured me, and I'm at his mercy. He says he'll let me go if I beg him to take his...

Eager Housewife

Her best friend's dad is advertising for a free use convenient housewife, and she's the perfect applicant.

Forbidden Employees

Kingpin's Nanny

My grumpy boss bought my whole evening as a camgirl!

Bratva's Secret Girl

She's my secret obsession. Then they find her.